# Murder in
# Mexico

# THE SPY WHO WASN'T THERE 2

# Murder in
# Mexico

## CORA TAYLOR

COTEAU
BOOKS
FOR KIDS

Edited by Geoffrey Ursell.
Cover image: "Uxmal," Photodisc Photography/Veer.
Models photographed by Austring Photography Ltd.
Interior maps by Dawn Pearcey.
Cover montage and design by Duncan Campbell.
Book design by Karen Steadman.
Printed and bound in Canada by Gauvin Press.

**Library and Archives Canada Cataloguing in Publication**

Taylor, Cora, 1936-
    Murder in Mexico / Cora Taylor.

(The spy who wasn't there ; 2)
ISBN 1-55050-353-7

    I. Title. II. Series: Taylor, Cora, 1936- . Spy who wasn't there ; 2.
PS8589.A883M87 2006      jC813'.54      C2006-904568-2


10  9  8  7  6  5  4  3  2  1

2517 Victoria Ave
Regina, Saskatchewan
Canada   S4P 0T2

*available in Canada and the US from:*
Fitzhenry & Whiteside
195 Allstate Parkway
Markham, Ontario
Canada   L3R 4T8

The publisher gratefully acknowledges the financial assistance of the Saskatchewan Arts Board, the Canada Council for the Arts, the Government of Canada through the Book Publishing Industry Development Program (BPIDP), the Association for the Export of Canadian Books and the City of Regina Arts Commission, for its publishing program.

*This one is for the Livingstons:*
*son Clancy, Jane and, of course, Dylan!*

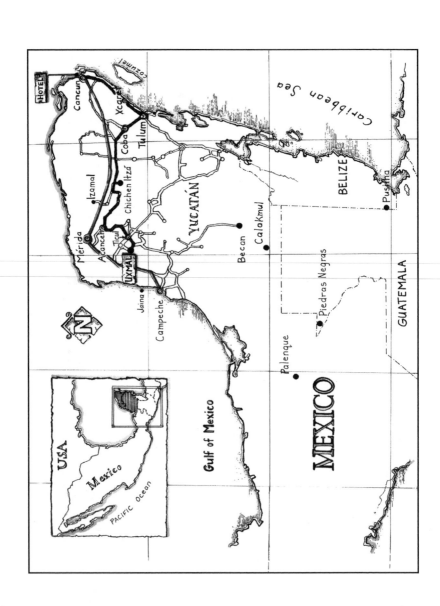

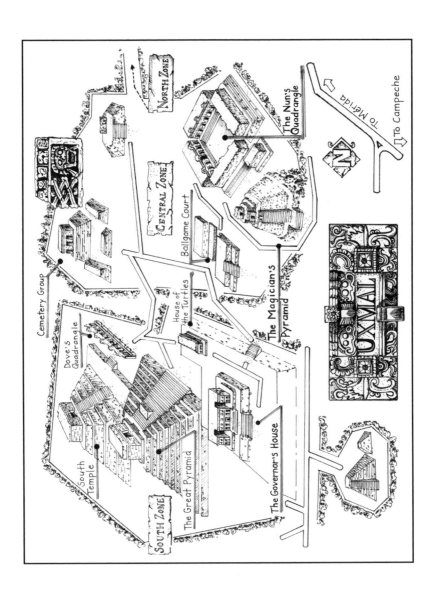

NORTH ZONE

The Nun's Quadrangle

To Mérida

To Campeche

N

CENTRAL ZONE

Ballgame Court

The Magician's Pyramid

Cemetery Group

House of the Turtles

Dove's Quadrangle

South Temple

SOUTH ZONE

The Great Pyramid

The Governor's House

UXMAL

"**I**sn't it about time we switched seats again?" Maggie asked.

Jennifer knew better than to pretend that she didn't know or to say it wasn't time. That would have been a lie, and Jennifer had to watch that. Ever since she'd found the old parchment and tried the invisibility spell even the tiniest fib would cause her to disappear. Not exactly a good thing to happen on a crowded airliner.

"I guess so," she said. "Whose turn is it to have the window seat now?"

Jennifer couldn't wait for the plane to land in Cancun. Maggie was driving her crazy. If she had to listen to one more historical fact about the Mayans, the Toltecs, the Olmecs and any of the other -ecs who had once lived in Mexico, she would take violent action.

She was almost desperate enough to change seats even if it meant that she wouldn't be able to watch them come in to land.

All the way from Edmonton they had switched seats every hour. Maggie had actually made a schedule before they left. A Maggie sort of thing to do. At first it seemed ridiculous to have a seating plan, but Jennifer had to admit that it saved a lot of squabbling. Her twin sister was definitely the practical one.

Right now their friend and next-door-neighbour, Samuel Elwin, was on the aisle, with Maggie in the middle. Jennifer had realized early in the flight that the arrangement she preferred was the one where she had the window and Sam sat in the middle. Less chance of sisterly conflict.

Sam actually seemed to enjoy Maggie's lectures, but after all, he was travelling with his grandfather, who was an archaeologist. He'd be visiting Sayil, a Mayan site in Yucatan province. Some colleagues of Dr. Martell's were excavating there and Sam and Dr. Martell would be staying at the Dig. But before that her grandmother was going to be taking the three of them on a little sight-seeing tour. To listen to Maggie, it would be exclusively old Mayan temples, pyramids and palaces, but Jennifer figured there'd be time for beaches and swimming in the Gulf of Mexico and the Caribbean Sea. Thanks to Maggie and Sam she already knew that the Yucatan peninsula touched on both. As long as the water was warm and the beaches were as beautiful as everyone said, that was enough for Jennifer.

She peered past Maggie and Sam across the aisle to where Grand was sitting with Dr. Martell.

It was great to have a grandmother who'd take them on a holiday like this. They'd travelled with her once before on a Greek cruise. That had been more than just a holiday. It had really been to rescue their father. Definitely one of the most exciting things that had ever happened to Jennifer. And the happiest – at least for herself and Maggie. Sam, she thought, would probably never forget it either. After all he'd almost been shot by a spy.

No worries this time. Dad was safely back in Canada flying for Air Canada out of Vancouver. And Mum was teaching at home in Edmonton. Or she would be again once Spring Break was over. Meantime it was nice that she'd agreed that the girls could spend another holiday with their father's mother. A real holiday this time. No spies. No rescues.

Jennifer sighed. She'd rather liked the excitement. She probably wouldn't even need to become invisible on this trip, though she had no intention of ruling it out. After all, she did enjoy bugging Maggie by vanishing on her now and then.

Going through the Airport in Cancun was fairly easy, Sam thought. There was a long line-up, of course, but the Customs and Immigration part hadn't taken too long. You just stood there and when your turn came, you pushed a button – if the traffic light above was green you marched through – if it came up red you had to go into another line and it took a little longer. Everybody came up green but Jennifer.

"Do you think they'll decide to keep her?" Maggie asked, rolling her eyes.

Sam laughed. He knew Maggie meant that if they kept Jennifer they'd be sorry. He didn't say anything. Sometimes he walked a fine line between the twins and it didn't pay to take sides. They stood waiting for Jennifer to join them.

"Did they have fun searching your suitcase?" Maggie asked, looking innocent. "I hope they didn't muss things up!"

Jennifer just glared. Sam turned his head to hide his smile – nobody could mess up a suitcase Jennifer had packed. He'd seen her. She crammed it so full she had to sit on it to close it. He felt sorry for the Mexican security person who'd had to tangle with that. It had probably popped open like a Jack-in-the-Box, spewing hats and bathing suits all over the counter.

They ran the gauntlet of people in the airport, offering everything from car rentals to Time-Share viewing. The girls' grandmother had ordered a Budget rent-a-car ahead of time. Grandad was staying overnight with them, and tomorrow someone from the Dig would pick him up. After five days of sight-seeing with Mrs. Arnold and the girls, Sam would join his grandfather at Sayil. He was looking forward to it. He'd be helping. Not exactly a summer job – Grandad was paying him – but he'd be on a real archeological dig, staying on an extra week after Spring Break. It would be great experience. No promises had been made, in fact it hadn't even been mentioned, but Sam was hoping this would lead to working on excavations with Grandad during his summer holidays from now on.

Jennifer was the first one out of the car at the hotel. Las Perlas looked exotically Mexican, with coral adobe walls and tile roof. She waited impatiently for their respective grandparents to check in, then grabbed the key to their room and ran ahead.

"Last one on the beach is a rotten egg!"

No point in trying to compete. When he and Grandad went into their room, he rushed to the balcony. Below them the swimming pool rippled in the sunshine, and beyond that a beautiful beach waited. Waves were lapping on the sand, and behind the wharf restaurant someone zipped by on a sailboard. Sam only gazed for a minute; at least it seemed like only a minute, but below him a tangled head of long brown hair dashed past the swimming pool heading for the water. Unmistakably Jennifer.

He met Maggie on the stairs. She was carrying a beach ball, a bag with sun tan lotion and two beach towels. Obviously, Jennifer had forgotten hers.

Jennifer was already splashing about in the roped off area on the beach. The rotten eggs joined her.

**T**hat night they had dinner at Carlos & Charlie's. Jennifer already had the makings of a sunburn. The only thing, Sam thought, that had saved her was not Maggie's lotion but the fact that they'd arrived so late in the day.

The restaurant was on the lagoon-side of the Boulevard Kukulcan, the road running along the strip of hotels and tourist places. Maggie was studying the little road map of Cancun in the coupon booklet they'd picked up at the airport. They each had one.

"Look, Grand!" Maggie pointed, "there's a Museum down on the strip."

Jennifer rolled her eyes. "Bathroom!" she said. "Try to finish yacking about the museum by the time I get back."

Sam watched her orange hat with the sunflower bobbing away past the bar. Good. He could agree with Maggie without bugging Jennifer. And they had finished their "museum talk" by the time the sunflower reappeared among the tables.

"Guess what!" Jennifer demanded instant attention. "Talk about 'small world' and all that stuff...you'll never guess who I saw at the bar!"

She had his and Maggie's attention all right. She leaned forward conspiratorially. "I just saw Mr. Brady!"

Her grandmother's head turned to Jennifer so quickly, Sam feared she'd have whiplash. "You don't mean...."

"Yep! The very same man."

Sam could tell Jennifer was enjoying every minute of this. And he had to admit it was big news. Brady had been the CIA operative who'd saved his life on board the *Stella Solaris* when a double agent was holding him at gun point, trying to find out where they'd hidden the girls' father.

Nobody had a chance to say anything. Grand was looking very serious, throwing rapid-fire questions at Jennifer. "Was he alone? Did he see you? What did he say?"

For all her dash-about ways, Jennifer could be very precise when she had to be. Sam had seen it before, but it always surprised him.

"Nobody sitting beside him. He saw me all right. Looked straight at me...straight *through* me...didn't say a word." Jennifer looked at Grand and didn't give her a chance to ask another question. "I didn't say anything either. Pretended I didn't know him. I figured he might be on assignment and wouldn't want to have his cover blown," she finished smugly.

Grand nodded approvingly. "Very wise, my dear, I'm sure." Her brow creased and she shook her head. "I'm puzzled," she said. "I would have supposed his assignment was the Middle East."

She looked at the three young people in turn. "I think we should all follow Jennifer's lead and just ignore Mr. Brady unless he speaks to one of us." She picked up the menu. "Anyone for dessert? Other than Jennifer?"

When they left and walked past the crowded bar, there was no sign of Mr. Brady.

"I should have become invisible last night and gone right back to the bar to see who he was waiting for." Jennifer mumbled. "Someone probably showed up and he left with him."

"Or her," said Sam.

"What does it matter," Maggie said impatiently. "Who cares? And it's none of our business. Maybe spies get to take vacations too." She wished Jennifer would just drop it. It *was* none of their business. The last thing they needed was to get mixed up in another spy adventure. Why couldn't Jennifer just relax and enjoy being in this beautiful place?

"Wow, look at that big blue one!" Sam said pointing down.

They were standing on the boardwalk surrounding the restaurant on the dock, feeding the last of their breakfast toast to the fishes. Brilliantly coloured fish darted about in the water beneath them. The big blue one had just scattered some of the round angel-fish-shaped yellow ones. There were long, almost eel-like ones with stripes and great long snouts that Sam said might be some kind of gar.

"I'm going back in to get some more bread." Jennifer looked at Maggie as if daring her to object. "The grandparents are still dawdling over coffee, so it'll be all right."

Sometimes, Maggie thought, she reads my mind. She watched as Jennifer dashed along the dock, almost bumping into a couple of men carrying pails and ropes. The men ignored them as they passed by, out to where the boats were moored. All kinds of craft were tied there, everything from small outboard-motor boats to larger ones with cabins. Even a few elegant sailboats. Maggie promised herself she'd keep an eye on the sailboats if anyone boarded them. She loved to see them unfurl their sails and skim across the water.

Sam nodded toward the men who'd passed them, now stowing their load onto a rather impressive launch. They were well out of ear-shot, but he spoke out of the side of his mouth. "Get a load of that guy in the cap...the one with the moustache...he must be expecting it to be cold out on the water."

Sam was right. The man was wearing a heavy jacket. On his head was a black knitted cap, not a toque, but close-fitted like a skullcap. It seemed very inappropriate attire for the day. Already, at eight in the morning, the sun was beating down. Maggie made a note to put extra lotion in her beach bag.

"Funny," Sam said, "those two don't look rich enough to own a boat like that."

He was staring down at the fish as he said it, but Maggie knew it was just part of the detective thing he and Jennifer did. Like speaking out of the side of their mouths when they commented to each other. They'd been doing this since they were kids, and she wished they'd give it a rest. It was one thing to pretend to be sleuths when you are ten years old, but at fourteen she'd hoped they'd have outgrown it. The childhood idea of having a detective agency when they grew up seemed to be even stronger since the trip to Greece and Turkey last year. She wasn't about to play along. After all, except for the men raking the beach in front of the hotel bar and rearranging the beach chairs, there wasn't a soul around to care whether she and Sam noticed the men on board. She stared straight at them as they moved about stowing things on the yacht.

"Well," she said dismissively, "it's probably much colder once they get out."

"Maybe," Sam sounded doubtful. He was still staring at the fish below. "But the other guy is dressed in a T-shirt and shorts. You don't think they're going to the same place?"

"Maybe the guy with the moustache has a cold or something," Maggie was getting impatient with this. She was relieved when Jennifer came clumping along the boards toward them.

"Hey Sam!" she said, handing Maggie a piece of bread. "You'd better go say 'good-bye' to your grandad. He and Grand are going to the lobby to wait for his friend to come and take him to Sayil." Jennifer giggled. "Did you know it means 'Place of the Ants' in Mayan? Hope they're not the killer kind, Sam," she called after him as he left.

Maggie broke up the bread, and she and Jennifer fed the fish in silence. She wasn't about to mention the man in the woolen hat to Jennifer. She watched though – she really expected a couple of well-dressed tourist types to come along and board the yacht, but just as she threw down the last of her bread she heard a motor start and the fancy white cruiser roared away out into the Gulf of Mexico.

**J**ennifer was relieved to find that Grand's driving had improved since the wild ride in the taxi they'd stolen in Istanbul. Not exactly "stolen." After all, the taxi driver had tried to kidnap them and he *was* along, even though they'd locked him in the trunk. The rented green Toyota was an easier car to drive, she guessed. Grand didn't have to shift gears, which made for a much smoother ride.

But, like Istanbul, Grand didn't know where they were going, and they got lost.

"This looks very familiar," Sam said diplomatically as they came to the same traffic circle off the highway between Cancun and Tulum.

They were headed for the pyramids at Coba, but the sign seemed uncertain as to whether they should go half-way around the traffic circle or three-quarters of the way. They'd now tried both those exits and had had to turn back.

"If at first you don't succeed..." Grand said, driving back around and taking what would have been the first one as you entered the circle on the road from Highway 307.

Soon they were driving past a busy town site.

"*Topes!*" yelled Jennifer, and Grand stepped on the brakes just in time.

They'd already learned to recognize "*Topes*" signs that warned of the large bumps slowing traffic in the villages. Hit one of those at more than 5 kilometres an hour and you risked losing your muffler *and* your passengers' teeth.

"*Topes*" was the only Spanish word Jennifer ever used. Unlike Maggie, who carried a phrase book and liked to pepper her conversation with "*por favor*" and "*gracias*" even when there was nobody Mexican around. Maggie claimed it was all part of her plan to be fluent in several languages so she could be a diplomat someday. Jennifer had hoped she'd get over it, but it seemed to be getting worse.

"The site of Coba dates from A.D. 613 to 780," Maggie was reading from the guide book – as usual – as they walked along the path past the admission stand.

"You might just as well have stayed home and read the guide book, Muggins." Jennifer grumbled, "You're missing everything!" Under her breath she added. "I hope she walks into a tree."

Trees lined the path and hid the sky above them. A real jungle. Jennifer craned her neck to look into the branches above.

"Look Sam!" A beautiful yellow-breasted bird with black and white on its wings and back landed just above her. "What's that?"

They stepped off the trail and Sam pulled his *Bird Watcher's Guide to Mexico* out of his backpack. "Abeille's Oriole," he said pointing to the picture.

Maggie had actually taken her eyes off the guide book. "Yes, that must be the one...there's a nest hanging over there!"

They arrived at the first building complex. Amazing to see these massive buildings appear suddenly in the jungle, Jennifer thought.

"L'Iglesia was so called because the human figure on the stelae in front reminded people of a virgin statue. This complex (known as 'Coba') has a very well-preserved ball court with rings still in place," read Maggie.

"Oh, that's interesting," said Sam. "Remember all the ball court rings in the Museum? I didn't think we'd be lucky enough to see some *in situ*."

Jennifer resisted the impulse to tell Sam to stop talking like an archeologist just because he'd be spending a week or so brushing the dirt off some old stones with a paintbrush. She decided to climb up the stone steps and explore inside some of the passages in the building. It did look a little like a church. The sun was beating down, and even though she'd worn her coolest top and shorts, it didn't feel so great with her sunburn. Her sunflower hat was hot, too, even though it protected her from the sun. Grand had insisted she wear it – "So I can find you when you roam away from the other two."

Her head was throbbing from the heat by the time she entered the hallway beside the steps. She stood for a minute to let her eyes get accustomed to the gloom. It was much cooler – damp, but cool. She stared at the walls to see if there were any of the Puuc style carvings Sam was always going on about. It would be good to see the looks on their faces if she found something they hadn't seen.

Peering at the stones, it took her a minute or so to notice that there was someone at the other end of the tunnel-like passage, then she could see that there were two people. A couple of other tourists, she thought, but then as the men emerged into the sunlight she recognized one of them. Brady. Now she wished she'd moved through more quickly. The other man turned the corner too fast for her to see much of him. Brady had paused and looked back down the tunnel and then moved quickly away in the opposite direction.

Jennifer was sure he wouldn't have recognized her; after all, she would have been just a dim form in the passage with the light behind her. Except, she realized, for the hat. She'd been wearing it the other night too. She snatched it off her head and ran after the two men, but when she rushed out into the sunlight there was no sign of either of them. Hard to believe they could have disappeared so quickly, although the man with Brady might be in that group of tourists walking through the ball court now. She hadn't seen enough of him to recognize him. Brady had gone the other direction and had somehow managed to vanish into the jungle.

But now she saw Maggie and Sam just leaving the ball court and dashed after them.

"Did you see anyone...a man join the group behind you a minute ago?"

Both shook their heads impatiently.

"Come on, Grand's waiting..." Maggie gave her a look. "Where did you disappear to anyway?"

Jennifer didn't answer. She could see Grand talking to a man beside some bicycle-type rickshaws.

"Eulogio and his friend are going to take us around the site," she said as they came up to her. "This site is a bit large for walking...70 square kilometres...so even with the rickshaws we won't see all of it, but we can see the Nohochmul pyramid. I don't think we should miss that."

"Definitely not," Maggie interrupted. "It's the highest pyramid in the Yucatan peninsula...higher than the Temple of the Magician at Uxmal or the Castle at Chichen Itza."

Grand laughed at her. "Very good, Maggie. It's 42 metres high." She nodded towards the man who was waiting to peddle their rickshaw, "And Eulogio speaks Mayan. He's from the village nearby. The name means Big Hill. He says *'Nohoch'* is 'big' and *'Mal'* is 'hill'."

Jennifer was impressed in spite of herself. A real Mayan. Probably his great-great-great – better add few hundred greats – had lived in this city and played in the ball courts for real. She was glad that she'd be sharing the rickshaw with Grand.

Sam and Maggie were getting Eulogio's friend to pedal them and be their tour guide. She wondered if their man spoke English as well as Eulogio. Just in case, she decided to wait and tell Grand about Brady later.

"Do you mind if I put my hat in your carry-all, Grand?" she asked. "It's really hot. I think I'll risk sunstroke for a while. And," she teased, "you're not likely to lose me when I'm sitting right beside you!"

Jennifer didn't want Brady to spot her too easily, and she was determined to keep an eye out in case he reappeared.

**B**umping along in the rickshaw, Maggie decided, was only slightly better than walking, but even on the jungle trail with the tall trees protecting her from the sun, the heat was beginning to get to her. She was tempted to borrow Jennifer's hat, since it seemed Jen had decided to take it off.

They got to "The Paintings," a moderate sized pyramid with a small structure on top where coloured material still showed. She and Sam decided to climb up.

"Okay if I borrow your hat?" she asked Jennifer.

"Go ahead...Grand's got it...but you'll be hot!"

Jennifer was pulling her detective/spy routine with Sam while Maggie went to Grand to get the hat. She pulled the hat on and realized Jen was right – it was fabric, not straw, so it didn't take long for Maggie's short hair to be soaked with perspiration. Still, she hoped it would keep her from sunstroke while they climbed.

To her amazement, Jennifer decided she wouldn't go with them.

"What's Jennifer on about now?" she asked Sam as they began to climb the crumbling stones.

Sam looked back down towards the rickshaws where Grand was talking to Eulogio and fanning herself with a map of the site. He was obviously checking to see if they could be overheard. Maggie groaned inwardly.

"She saw Brady at L'Iglesia," Sam said out of the side of his mouth, "but he disappeared by the time she got out of the passage. I said we'd see if we could see him from the top. She's going to wander a little."

Maggie was tired and could feel the sweat running down the back of her neck. She wished she hadn't borrowed the stupid hat.

Sam grinned at her. "She was glad you wore the hat. You can be the decoy...in case he turns up. He won't suspect she's watching!"

Maggie was tempted to rip the hat off and stomp back down, but they were at the top now.

An effort had been made to protect the stelae and bits of paint on it. There was a thatched *palapa* cover. Sam took several pictures. He held up the digital camera to show her, and she was surprised that she could actually make out some figures on the viewer.

Up here the sun beat down mercilessly. She'd hoped for a bit of breeze, but the air lay flat and heavy and unbearably hot. Sam seemed to be unaware. Now he was using his zoom lens and taking shots of all the people on the trail below. She could just make out Grand with Eulogio and Jennifer lurking behind a tree as a new group of tourists came along the path.

"I'm going," she said impatiently and started down. Luckily, it didn't seem to take as long going down. She got rid of the hat as soon as she was in the shade with Grand.

"Where's Jennifer?" she asked. "When I looked down from the pyramid she was with you."

Grand was still fanning herself with the guide map, looking hot and tired. "She said she was going to go back to the little kiosk and get me a bottle of water. I probably shouldn't have let her go, but it seemed like a good idea at the time."

"What's the next stop?" Maggie asked Eulogio.

"There's another ball court not far away." He and his companion were waiting patiently for the tour to continue.

Maggie could see Sam leaving the bottom of the pyramid. "Come on Sam!" she called. "We'll go and see that, and Grand and Jennifer can catch up."

"A good idea...and if we don't, you could come back this way and find us." Grand smiled.

One side of the ball court was very well preserved; one side overgrown and the ring broken. What made it different was that this one had a carving of a jaguar, like a manhole cover, on the floor at one end. Sam was busy taking pictures. He even took one of Maggie's foot beside the carving. "Gives perspective," he explained.

This time Maggie was tempted to whisper out of the side of her mouth. "Jennifer told Grand she was going back to get her a bottle of water," she told Sam. "A lie, or what?" Maggie felt annoyed, and it wasn't just the heat. "She's not going to do an invisible thing and try to follow Brady, is she?" She groaned. "If he is here on assignment, she could mess things up and get in serious trouble...."

"...and if he isn't?" Sam was looking at her quizzically.

"Then, I guess she'll just be her usual pain-in-the-butt!" She had to laugh. She really shouldn't take her sister so seriously. Go with the flow, as Grand said.

Sam was taking a close-up of the jaguar. "I got one of you and your grandmother when I was coming down from the pyramid. Wanna see?"

Maggie leaned over the camera as Sam pressed buttons. The picture of her and Grand flashed by before he could stop. There was a shot of Jennifer heading down the trail. Sam had used the zoom lens and Maggie could see clearly. There was a man – Brady, probably. Up ahead of Jennifer, and leaning against a tree looking as if he was in the same group of people, was a moustached man wearing a little woolen hat.

"Stop, Sam!" Maggie pointed to the picture. "It can't be, can it?"

"If it is, it's a very strange coincidence." But he turned and hurried to Eulogio and the waiting bicycle. "I think we should get back," he said. And out of the side of his mouth, "There are probably several men in Mexico who have moustaches and that sort of hat."

Somehow that made Maggie feel more uneasy than if Sam had been convinced it was the same man. Was he just trying to distract her? It wasn't like the Big Detective to not follow up a clue like that.

**G**rand was still waiting and there was no sign of Jennifer.

"We might as well head back," she said. "We'll probably meet her coming back along the trail.

Sam wasn't sure. What if Jennifer had managed to become invisible? They had to hope that she would see them and make contact. Sometimes he wished she'd plan ahead a little.

Eulogio stopped on the way showing them a bee tree. He even let the bees crawl over his arm. Nice bees. Obviously not the famous killer ones. It was interesting, but Sam was more interested in what might have become of Jennifer.

Then they stopped to look at the remains of the road bed that had connected Coba to Chichen Itza.

"Amazing!" Maggie was into the guide book again. "The road," she said, her voice rising in amazement, "is one hundred miles long." She took her nose out of the book long enough to study the impressive stonework. "Wow!"

Sam was impressed too, but he wanted to keep moving.

Where was Jennifer? They were almost to the place where they had rented the bicycle rickshaws. The path forked here and turned back to the entrance or went over to L'Iglesia. There was no sign of her.

She could be invisible of course. Sam braced himself at the thought. Jennifer would, no doubt, announce her presence with a sharp poke in the ribs. It was always hard to maintain proper detective composure when that happened. Especially if she took him by surprise.

But there were no jabs or pokes or voices in thin air. Nothing happened – nothing at all.

They thanked Eulogio and his friend and started back toward the entrance kiosks. Grand was looking worried.

Maggie was unperturbed, her nose in the guidebook. "Although the site at Coba was used between 975 and 1200, it remained occupied until the 16th Century". She looked up laughing, "I'd say it still is...after all, Eulogio and his family are still here!"

"Yes, dear," Grand said absently, trying to see through the group of tourists at the kiosk ahead.

"There she is!" Sam was more relieved than he wanted to admit when he saw Jennifer emerge from the head of the line.

She was carrying a bottle of water and she looked very upset.

Grand said, "Thank you, Dear!" and reached for the bottle.

Jennifer didn't even seem to notice. She grabbed Sam's arm and pulled him back.

"What happened?" Sam was really alarmed. Jennifer was forever doing crazy things but she rarely lost her cool. Had Brady spotted her? Had she learned something that would put her in danger? "Are you okay?"

Jennifer glared. "I'm fine..." she said, "just fine...too flippin' fine!"

Sam wasn't sure how to decipher that but he was relieved anyway. If Jennifer was cheesed off like this it wasn't likely to be anything life-threatening.

She stopped dead on the trail and looked at him. "It doesn't work!" She looked as if she might cry. "The spell doesn't work anymore." she moaned. "I lied and it didn't work!"

Sam didn't say anything. This was bad news. Bad news for their spying adventures, bad news for the future detective agency, but mostly bad news for Jennifer who'd incorporated this new "talent" into her life.

Maybe that was the problem. Maybe she'd over-used the ability to become invisible – worn it out or something. There had been frivolous use. He and Maggie had worried about that and insisted Jennifer stop playing tricks on kids at school she didn't like. But he remembered the last time she'd used it. They'd used it.

Mr. Wendel, their principal, had decided that it would be a good idea if, after the January exams, they had some entertainment. So he'd organized a talent contest. Even got some very impressive prizes donated from local businesses. As a result, instead of just the usual competitors who actually had talent there were a lot more who didn't. Kids who got together and decided to do skits or just about anything, hoping to get one of the lesser prizes.

He and Jennifer and Maggie had been one of the latter group. Jennifer's idea, of course. Sam had been "Samson the Amazing" – a magician. After his initial resistance to the idea, he'd actually got into the part and had begun to enjoy it.

"Ladies and gentlemen! Observe the parasol my assistant, the Lovely Maggie, is holding! Watch how, at my command, it will move across the stage to my hand!"

And, of course, the frilly pink parasol Sam had filched from his mother's Klondike Days costume, and which perfectly matched Maggie's pink swim suit draped with scarves, had floated across the stage, courtesy of an invisible Jennifer.

Everybody was very impressed by that. Even more so when he'd invited one of the teachers up and had them hold an empty Coca-Cola glass and, at a wave of Sam's wand, Coke had mysteriously begun to pour from mid-air into the glass.

A few more tricks like that – a feather boa appearing from nowhere around Maggie's neck and Sam's magician top hat being knocked off and replaced by a cowboy hat – and the audience was definitely amazed. Sam could taste victory.

If only they hadn't decided to have a rabbit.

They had learned that the way Jennifer's invisibility operated was that anything she was holding or wearing when she became invisible disappeared with her but reappeared if she let go or dropped the item. Anything she picked up afterwards just looked as if it was suspended in mid-air. So the parasol would float across the stage. The Coke, the boa, the cowboy hat, and other things would suddenly appear when she let go of them.

The problem with their act was that by the time Jennifer was loaded down with all the things they planned to use, the only place to stuff the rabbit was inside her T-shirt.

When Jennifer first used the Spell, she'd said the words. But then, to their horror, she'd disappear without it. It had taken them a while to figure out that lying made her vanish, and it had taken even longer to learn that laughing made her reappear.

And a wiggling bunny inside your shirt tickles.

Sam knew they were in trouble when he heard a disembodied giggle as he was removing the cowboy hat and bowing to the audience. He knew it wasn't Maggie, though she'd realized what was happening and moved over right away. And giggled.

Luckily, Jennifer managed to hide in the curtains while she became visible again.

The rest of the act was a disaster. Sam had already announced that he was going to pull a rabbit out of his hat. But, of course, there was no rabbit. Finally Maggie had reached into the curtain and retrieved the rabbit from Jennifer and stood holding it up behind Sam as he shook, tapped, and thumped the hat in vain. Fortunately, the audience thought the comedy ending was part of the act. They'd won a $50 gift certificate from HMV, their favourite record store at West Edmonton Mall.

Sam was smiling as he remembered.

"It's not funny," Jennifer snapped. "I told Grand I was going to get her a bottle of water and then set off to follow Brady." They were walking again now. Jennifer earnestly explaining. "I followed a ways behind, keeping an eye on my feet because they go first...well that and my fingers and hands...and ready to duck behind a tree so that I could vanish completely...and...." She sounded ready to cry again.

"But..." Sam couldn't help being puzzled. "You just handed your grandmother a bottle of water. It wasn't a lie after all!"

Jennifer looked at him. "But I didn't *mean* to get the bottle of water, I meant to follow Brady. It was just because he got in line that I had to...." She stopped. "I'm doomed!" she said dramatically. "I can't even lie properly!"

"It *is* strange," Sam conceded. "It means that the intention to lie is not enough...the Spell sees beyond that." They had caught up to Grand and Maggie now. "It poses an interesting philosophical question."

"A philosophical question?" Maggie perked up. "What's that, Sam?"

"When is a lie not a lie?"

**J**ennifer glared at them. "Very funny, you two."
She stomped off down the trail after Grand. It didn't help one bit to hear them discussing things like "the importance of intention" and "accidental outcome" as if it was some question on an exam. This was serious. She had lied. Intentionally. And if the spell had worked and she'd become invisible she wouldn't have ended up getting the bottle of water. So what was going on?

She caught up to Grand in the parking lot.

"We'll have to start the car and wait outside until the air conditioning cools it off, I'm afraid," Grand said, unlocking the door gingerly. "You might be able to stand sitting on the seat but touching anything metal, like your seat belt, could burn."

They were standing there waiting when Sam and Maggie arrived.

"Wow," Sam laughed, "just like Edmonton in January...except we're cooling the car, not heating it!"

Jennifer was not amused. She glared at him. "I'm sitting in the back seat!"

She didn't want to talk to any of them. She had some thinking to do. Ignoring Maggie's shocked look, she opened the door and flopped into the seat. Big mistake. She sat on the metal end of the seat belt and nearly screamed. Obviously she should have waited outside the car longer, as the others were doing. She'd probably be branded just below her shorts like some doggie out on the Alberta range. It definitely didn't improve her mood.

"Look, Sam!" Maggie was saying as they climbed into the car. "There's the guy with the little woolen hat at the Souvenir Stand. Do you think he's the one from Las Perlas?"

Jennifer's head snapped around in the direction Maggie was pointing. What was that all about? Nobody had told her there was someone else here that they'd seen before in Cancun. Was he tailing Brady or was Brady tailing him? The thought of another mystery almost made her forget her problem with the spell and the burnt leg. But she was still mad at the two of them for getting all philosophical about her invisibility problem, so she bit her lip and didn't ask.

Luckily, Grand did. "You mean that man who's looking at the carvings?" she asked. "It is a bit warm to be wearing a cap, but I suppose it's insulation against the heat as well as the cold. Does look odd though, I suppose. Not that he'd stand out much any more than the bearded man over there in the white hat and ponytail."

"I think it's the same man, Maggie," Sam said. "But I suppose that there are a lot of dark-looking Mexicans with bushy moustaches around. And some of them might even have little woolen skullcap-type hats."

"Yes," said Maggie, "but not all of them were watching Jennifer follow Mr. Brady."

"What!!" Grand swivelled around in her seat to look at Jennifer, which was too bad because she'd started to pull out of the parking lot and almost hit a tree. "Jennifer!" she said, slamming on the brakes just in time. "Don't tell me you were bothering poor Mr. Brady? The man could very well just be trying to have a vacation like anyone else and if he isn't...."

Her tone of voice left little doubt as to the seriousness of the situation. "You could jeopardize his job...and his life."

"We just happened to be going in the same direction," Jennifer said, though it sounded a bit lame even to her. "But what about the man in the hat?" She turned to Sam accusingly. "Have you two got a mystery going without me?"

"Not much," laughed Sam. "Man goes in swanky motor launch on hot day, inappropriately dressed. Hardly a mystery."

"But it *is* funny to see him here," said Maggie.

Jennifer suspected her sister was enjoying making her curious. Maggie wasn't likely to notice a mystery if she fell over it.

Jennifer was still feeling a bit sulky as they drove through the village. She didn't bother to yell "*Topes*" and Grand didn't brake in time. It gave her some satisfaction to see Sam bang his head on the ceiling of the car when they hit the bump too hard. She didn't appreciate being left out of things.

She had too much on her mind to worry very long about the man. They were probably making a big deal of him just to bug her. The spell. That was her big worry. Had it worn off? She remembered that they'd speculated in the very beginning that it might wear off, or have a limit on it somehow – like the magical three wishes in fairy tales.

There was only one thing to do. Try again. Next time she'd tell a whopper. Something that couldn't possibly be true. The thought cheered her up. She even managed to show some enthusiasm when a colourful toucan flew across the road in front of their car.

"Can you believe, I'll bet its bill is two-thirds the length of the whole bird, tail and all?" Maggie laughed.

Maybe Grand was looking too closely at the bush the bird had gone into or maybe the car was just going awfully fast but they had swerved dangerously close to the trees along the narrow road when a large black car came out of nowhere and passed them. The windows were tinted, but Jennifer was sure she saw a white hat inside.

They did not see Mr. Brady again until they were at Xcaret, the place people referred to as the Mexican Disneyland. This time he wasn't alone.

Maggie wasn't sure it should be called a "Disneyland," except for the fact that there was a lot of walking and you'd have trouble seeing everything in one trip. Xcaret had a personality all its own. There were no rides, for one thing, unless you wanted to count the *Papantla* "flyers"– performers who jumped and swung from the towers.

"What was your favourite part?" she asked Sam and Grand. They were sitting at a wonderful outdoor restaurant, waiting for the Mexican buffet to be ready.

Grand laughed as she raised her glass. "Well, this is certainly the best Margarita I've tasted since the ones at Casa di Pico in Old Town San Diego!"

Sam saluted her in return with his Coke, "I loved seeing the manatees when we walked down along the lagoon." He shook his head. "They're amazing creatures but I can't figure out why early sailors would confuse them with mermaids. Those guys must have been at sea a *very* long time!"

"I pick the Mayan Village." Maggie sipped her lemonade. "Just imagine those potters and weavers making things the same way as their ancestors did hundreds of years ago!"

Jennifer came to the table and flopped down. "I'm in love!" she said dramatically. "That black jaguar over there has the most magnificent head. And his eyes...just amazing. Hypnotic."

She grabbed at the binoculars around Sam's neck to look back toward the island where the two jaguars were lying, as he struggled to get the strap off over his head before she strangled him.

"Look at him!" she said, ignoring Sam, who was now rubbing his throat. "I had no idea they were so huge! No wonder the Mayans carved them everywhere. Come on, Sam...take a couple of pictures for me!"

Maggie came with them as they walked back to the railing.

"Don't go trying to get over the moat and visit him!" Maggie figured the jaguar was very safe. The moat was the deepest she'd ever seen. A sharp drop of rock on both sides completely encircled the cat island. People clustered along the railing to get a closer look.

Sam laughed. "She's not likely to do that. See there? Along the stream at the bottom? There's an alligator or cayman or something."

"Hmmm," Maggie said, "I wonder if it would notice someone invisible...." She wouldn't even have suggested it if she'd thought there was the remotest possibility that anyone could actually climb down. Far be it from her to put any ideas in Jennifer's head.

"Probably smell them...hunt them down...." Sam snapped his jaws and smacked his lips, getting into the spirit of things. Sam waited for Jennifer's reaction as they walked back to the table.

Jennifer didn't respond. She sat down, staring into the binoculars. Maggie was surprised to realize they weren't really pointed at the jaguars any more.

"It's Mr. Brady again, Grand," Jennifer said softly. "He's just coming around the far side. Coming this way. Maybe he *is* on vacation...."

Sam grabbed his binoculars back. "I see...hmmm...that's some beautiful señorita he's with."

Maggie was sorely tempted to demand a turn, but she could see Brady now too. The young woman with him was the sort that would turn heads all right. Any man with her would be noticed. Or maybe not, Maggie thought. Everyone would be busy watching her. She was wearing a white halter dress with a full skirt and white high-heeled sandals, her long dark hair swinging like the models in the shampoo ads on television.

"Great hair!" Maggie murmured.

"It's a wig, I'll bet!" Jennifer had wrestled the binoculars back from Sam again. "But get a load of that necklace! Shouldn't she get a fashion citation for wearing diamonds with a sundress?"

It did look odd, Maggie thought, although Jennifer was hardly the one to give out fashion citations when she still insisted on wearing that dreadful old sunflower hat from time to time.

"I suggest," Grand said quietly, "that we go and get in line for the buffet. It's very rude to be staring like this."

"Why not stare?" Jennifer giggled. "Everyone else is!" But she got up and followed Grand to the line-up.

Jen was right, Maggie thought. The glamorous señorita was getting as much attention as the jaguars now. She let Sam go first. She wanted to see the famous necklace. She hated to admit it, but Jennifer was probably right about it being diamonds. The necklace flashed in the sunlight every time the woman moved.

Maggie forced her eyes away to look at Brady. Remarkable. He seemed to be interested in the necklace too. More interested in it than in his dazzling companion.

Maggie didn't like buffets much. Not that she couldn't make choices, but she liked things to go together and she didn't like to mix the tastes. Especially when there were foods she didn't know if she'd like or not. Jennifer didn't have a problem. She just piled everything she came to on her plate until it was heaped and you couldn't tell what was what even if you had known to begin with.

When they returned to their table Brady and his bejewelled señorita were nowhere in sight, but there was someone they'd seen before seated a few tables away.

**T**he bearded man with the pony tail and white straw hat stood up and bowed as the girls' grandmother walked by. Mrs. Arnold acknowledged it with a gracious nod, but neither of them said a word. Curiouser and curiouser, Sam thought.

Evidently Jennifer and Maggie did too. They'd no sooner put their plates down and sat at the table than the whispered questions began.

"Do you know him, Grand?" from Jennifer.

"Who *is* that man?" Maggie persisted.

Their grandmother laughed. "No," she said, "I don't actually *know* him but of course I know *of* him. Don't you remember? I pointed him out to you at Coba the other day. That's the famous Greek tycoon, Elefterious Sko-pakos!"

"Never heard of him," said Sam. He had the feeling that the twins would be on this like orcs after hobbits.

"His yacht, the Agamemnon," Mrs. Arnold said, trying to hide a smile, "is probably cruising around the Caribbean and he's come ashore."

Sam was sure this last bit of information was a bit of a tease on the twins' grandmother's part just to incite even more interest. If it was, it certainly worked.

Jennifer was ignoring her meal altogether. "But," she whispered, almost sputtering with excitement, "he acted like he knew you!"

Maggie was evidently impressed too. "Right," she hissed, "that bow! Wow!"

Their grandmother seemed to have dismissed the whole thing and was concentrating on her food. "Oh," she said, "I'm sure that's just his way. He has quite a reputation with the ladies, I understand."

That, Sam thought, was hardly the way to stop Jennifer and Maggie. In fact it would just serve to whet their interest more. They might not always work as a team but when they did, look out! Questions were flying thick and fast. He concentrated on his meal. He decided to eat quickly and go and get a few pictures of the jaguar and its "hypnotic eyes" until the twins settled down a bit.

He had just left the table when he noticed Brady walking back up the trail. He was alone now. Sam stood back and waited until he went by. Neither spoke nor acknowledged the other. Brady was headed for the Butterfly House, as far as Sam could see. He'd been that way and there was nothing else in that direction. The path came to a dead end.

He wasn't the first to see the body in the moat, but almost. A woman ahead of him looked over the railing and screamed.

It wasn't a place people usually stood at the railing. It was near where the island was divided between the jaguars and other cats, so people just moved along and didn't look down.

Now Sam did. He looked to where the screaming woman was pointing. A white dress flared around legs and bare feet. He could see the beautiful hair spread against a rock. Strange...it was too far from the body. Had the woman somehow been decapitated in the fall? He wished he had his binoculars, but he hadn't managed to get them back from Jennifer before he left the table. He realized he did have his camera – he could use the zoom. He hoped nobody would think he was ghoulish enough to be taking pictures. No one was looking at him anyway. All eyes were on the scene below.

Blood seemed to spread from the woman's head. A head that was still attached to her body. Jennifer had been right about the wig. The woman's head seemed to have been shaved, but it was not dark like the wig. It was short blondish-brown hair, cut like a man's. Sam could see her neck quite clearly lying at an unnatural angle. Her bare neck.

People had flocked to the railing now. He decided, almost as an afterthought, to snap one picture before someone was pushing him, trying to take his place at the railing. Jennifer, of course. He gave up without a struggle; he'd seen enough.

Sam felt dazed. He was vaguely aware of a couple of men in uniform rushing to the railing, attempting to move people away as he backed off. He stood staring back at the crowd still thick about the place where the woman must have fallen. On the ground not far from where Jennifer stood lay a white high-heeled sandal. He looked further along. The other one was being trampled by some of the crowd.

Do you kick off your shoes before you leap to your death? He wondered. The way you do before you dive into a pool? After you've removed your necklace? The whole thing was so bizarre, it gave him a feeling of unreality.

He turned back to the table. Mrs. Arnold was sitting there alone. Maggie must have gone to look as well. Most of the people who'd been sitting in the restaurant had left their meals and rushed to see what was going on, though beyond the girls' grandmother he could still see the white hat.

He wasn't sure how long it took him to get to the table. Everything he was doing felt as if it was slow motion, but he finally sat down.

"Drink this!" Mrs. Arnold was handing him a glass of iced tea. "I've put extra sugar in it," she said, "you look as though you're in a bit of shock." She looked towards the girls. "I wish those two would get back. They'll be cordoning off things. Possibly even closing this area." She rose from the table. "Stay here, Sam, I think I'd better fetch them."

Sam didn't have to be told; he had no desire to move. He sipped the tea. He didn't like it this sweet, but it did make him feel better.

Jennifer flopped down in her chair and looked at her uneaten food in disgust. "It was the woman who was with Brady." She paused dramatically. "She's dead!"

Maggie sat down. Unlike Jennifer, she seemed frozen into silence. Sam handed her the iced tea and she took it without a word and began to drink.

"I expect," said Mrs. Arnold. "That it would be sensible for us to leave as soon as we are allowed to do so. I'm not sure what police procedure is in Mexico in a case like this, but I expect they'll have enough Spanish-speaking witnesses. We might have to give our names and where we are staying though." She looked around.

"Have you paid *la cuenta*?" Maggie wasn't too dazed to practice her Spanish.

Her grandmother nodded.

People were leaving the area now, or just standing back watching to see what the security guards would do next. They could hear sirens in the distance. Police would be arriving.

"I don't think for a minute that she jumped!" Jennifer seemed to be the only one unaffected, Sam thought.

"We'll talk about it in the car, Jennifer!" Mrs. Arnold said firmly, getting up from the table. "For now we'll just follow those others who are leaving. I believe the main exit is this way."

The three of them followed. Even Jennifer was quiet but Sam could imagine what was going on in her mind. And *she* hadn't seen Brady coming back, going around the island. At least Sam was pretty sure she hadn't seen him. She'd have noticed the missing necklace though. Some time between them getting their food and eating it, that young woman had lost the diamond necklace and dropped into the chasm. And she hadn't screamed when she fell. How could that be?

It seemed strange to Sam how quickly they were back at the car. It had taken them hours coming in, but of course they'd been looking at the various displays of tropical birds and everything else. As they walked, he'd caught snatches of conversation from other people who'd been at the restaurant. Word had spread that it was suicide. Perhaps that was what the authorities thought too, since nobody stopped them to get names and addresses.

This time even Jennifer waited outside the car until the air conditioning had cooled it off. Nobody said a word all the way back. Now as they pulled out of the parking lot Jennifer finally did. But it wasn't the usual Jennifer exuberance from before.

"You know," she said softly almost to herself. "I don't think that señorita was a señorita."

Jennifer found the silence in the car very annoying. She wanted to talk. This was definitely a mystery and mysteries excited her. If Grand hadn't insisted on rushing them away she'd have tried to become invisible. Would it have done any good to hang around and watch when the police started investigating? She had to admit that she probably wouldn't have understood what anyone was saying.

Now Sam and Maggie were acting like zombies and Grand was glaring at the road as if it was an enemy. Jennifer had to admit that the concentration seemed to have improved her driving, though she suspected Grand had turned the wrong way when they hit the highway. They'd checked out of Las Perlas this morning. Grand had made reservations for tonight at the Mayaland hotel near Chichen Itza, but shouldn't they be going north to take the highway to Cancun?

She finally decided to speak up. "Grand," she said, pointing. "That sign says that we're heading for Tulum."

"Yes, dear," Grand said looking in the rear-view mirror. "I thought that we'd take the road across country past Coba. It's shorter and would be more interesting."

Grand didn't sound too convincing. It might be shorter, but they'd make better time on the highway. And why was she checking the mirror so much? Jennifer turned around to peer out the back window. Behind them a large black limousine was weaving in and out of traffic, gaining on them.

"That looks inviting," Grand was pointing to a tent-like roadside restaurant on the side of the highway. "Why don't we stop and have a bite to eat!" She didn't wait for anyone's response, just signalled, cut across traffic, and came to a screeching halt in the narrow parking space.

At least that seemed to shake Sam and Maggie out of their lethargy.

"But we just ate!" said Sam.

"Why here?" said Maggie.

Jennifer didn't say a word. She was watching the limo speed on by, wishing the windows weren't tinted and she could get a look inside.

"That's true," said Grand, "but we could have a washroom break and a soft drink. I did rush you away and I'm afraid once we leave the highway at Tulum and pass Coba there aren't any places to stop." She was already out of the car.

"We were being followed," Jennifer said out of the side of her mouth and climbed out her side. She did pause long enough to enjoy the look on Sam's face. Maybe he'd snap out of it now, and she'd have someone to talk to.

Maggie came back from the restroom, looking disgusted. She bought a bottle of water and poured a bit on her napkin to wash her hands. Jennifer decided she'd wait until Chichen Itza, no matter how long it took.

As soon as Grand left for the washroom, Jennifer moved to a table on the outside. "Sit over here, Sam," she said, loud enough for Maggie to hear. "We can watch the people in the shops across the highway. And," she added aside, "we'll be able to see if the limo comes back."

Sam moved obediently over, but Jennifer had no intention of talking about whether or not they were being tailed.

"I was right about one thing..." She whispered as Sam sat down across the table. "That beautiful hair was a wig!"

Sam shook his head looking puzzled. "Yes," he said, "but I still don't understand why someone would be pretending to be a woman...."

Jennifer was impatient. "But it was cover. Obviously the person was with Brady, being very obvious. Flaunting that necklace. They were probably trying to lure somebody..." her voice trailed off.

It was Sam's turn to look disgusted. "Then obviously the plan backfired...or do you think Brady's 'lady' suddenly became depressed enough to do a swandive into the ditch?"

Jennifer looked annoyed. "Oh, so we're down to the old: Did she jump or was she pushed?"

"There's a third possibility," Sam said. "Did you hear a scream?"

Jennifer's eyes opened wide. "Anybody would scream if they were pushed. I would, for sure."

Sam tried not to imagine the earth-shaking scream that Jennifer might manage in such a situation. "Right." He said. "The person was already knocked out...or dead."

Grand was returning to sit with Maggie, so Jennifer started to get up, swung around so her back was to the other table, and hissed in Sam's ear. "So the plan backfired. There's not a doubt in my mind that whoever it was, was killed for that diamond necklace. Somebody," she said fiercely, "is getting away with murder!"

Jennifer kept watching as they drove on, but there was no black limo anywhere to be seen.

**S**itting in the front seat, Maggie was aware that Sam and Jennifer were passing notes back and forth behind her. They each had notebooks that were supposed to be for interesting things they'd seen on the trip. Right now anyone would think that they were filling the pages in Jennifer's with facts about today's visit to Xcaret. Anyone who didn't know Jennifer, that is.

The book was being passed, added to and then passed back. Maggie glanced over at Grand to see if she'd noticed, but her grandmother was frowning, concentrating on the road. Come to think of it, Maggie realized, Grand was looking particularly grim. It was not like her. And they were going extremely fast. Maggie shifted so that she could see the speedometer. Oh, oh! Mexico used kilometers just like at home, not miles the way the U.S. did, and they were going at least twenty clicks over the speed limit! Maybe they'd just been edging up and Grand hadn't noticed. She'd better say something.

"Grand..." She said hesitantly, "Did you know you're speeding? Rather a lot..."

To her relief her grandmother seemed to snap out of her reverie, glancing quickly down. The car slowed noticeably.

"Sorry," Grand smiled a little, shaking her head as if she was embarrassed. "I've been a bit preoccupied, I guess."

Maggie waited. She was sure Grand had more to say. Out of the corner of her eye she could see the two in the back seat pause in their note writing.

When Grand continued, it seemed to Maggie that she was talking to herself. "Something about that episode doesn't make sense." She shook her head. "I don't like it. I don't want your holiday spoiled by a bunch of cloak & dagger events. And," she turned her head to glance at Jennifer, "I don't want you getting mixed up in anything Mr. Brady is involved in. Obviously it's dangerous...and not just for him!"

Jennifer took a breath as if she was going to say something but to Maggie's amazement she was silent. Even she must have realized Grand wasn't finished speaking.

"I'll hand it to you Jennifer..." Grand said, in a friendlier tone of voice, "I'm proud of you. You haven't messed about with the invisibility thing since we arrived. And I'm sure you've been tempted. Very commendable, dear girl!"

Maggie twisted around. She didn't want to miss the expression on Jennifer's face. The question was – would Jennifer confess to Grand that she'd tried and failed?

Sam was staring at Jennifer too. Maggie knew he wouldn't say anything. Neither would she. It was Jennifer's problem. Now was her chance to share it with Grand, but she didn't. She just hung her head, looking miserable and mumbled, "Ummm... thanks...I guess..."

Maggie was puzzled now. She could tell by Sam's face as they exchanged looks he was as surprised as she was by Jen's decision not to tell. Sometimes it amazed her that she hadn't managed to figure out her twin sister after all these years. Most of the time, but not always.

Grand seemed to relax even more once they were off the highway and headed north again. "I think," she said, "we'll go directly to the hotel and relax for a bit before dinner. I'd certainly like to put my feet up after all that walking today. These Dr. Scholl's sandals are very comfortable, but there's a limit even for them!" She looked over at Maggie. "Then in the morning, if nobody minds, we can have an early break-fast and get onto the site at Chichen Itza as soon as it opens. Before too many tour buses arrive."

Maggie was pleased that everyone agreed. She was able to relax and just gaze out the window as they sped along the narrow road. They seemed to be the only vehicle on it once they'd passed the turn-off to Coba. But it seemed Grand wasn't finished.

"Sam," Grand turned to look at him, "do you think you'd be able to print the pictures you took today? I'd like to have a look at them when we meet for something to eat before bedtime."

"I mostly took jaguar pictures for Jennifer," Sam said. "Except for the ones earlier in the day...and then one of whoever it was...the body...afterwards."

"Whatever you've got. I think we should all see them." Grand was frowning again. "There's no telling who might be in the background of your shots. We'll meet in my room around six."

Maggie knew that Grand had splurged and got herself a separate room this time instead of sharing with her twin granddaughters. And, of course, Sam had his own room thanks to his Grandad. Naturally she was stuck with Jennifer but she was pretty sure that Jen would be plotting something with Sam so she was hoping to have a bit of peaceful time to herself.

"And, Sam," Grand's voice was deadly serious, "since we don't know what's going on, or exactly who's involved, be careful with those pictures. I wouldn't want anyone to see that you've got them. Even if we don't think they're important, they might be. Or someone might think they are. Do you understand?"

Maggie looked back. Sam was nodding, looking up at Grand's reflection in the rear view mirror. Jennifer, for once, looked nervous. Grand's mood seemed to have impressed everyone.

"One thing, about tomorrow." Grand added. "We stay together. And, if anyone sees anyone or anything suspicious, tell me immediately! And," again the deadly serious tone, "no wandering off becoming invisible, Jennifer." She twisted around to give her grand-daughter a look, then turned back smiling, "At least not without telling me!"

Maggie waited. This was an even better chance for Jen to confess she was having problems with the Spell. But Jennifer was staring out of the window. "Yes, Grand!" was all she said.

The rest of the drive was uneventful. They met one ramshackle truck and Maggie looked in vain for a toucan, though she did see two brilliant yellow and blue birds she thought might be parakeets. Unfortunately she'd put the bird book in her backpack in the trunk.

In the back seat, Jennifer and Sam scribbled busily and passed the notebook back and forth. Never mind, Maggie thought, she'd figure out a way to read those notes. She'd just wait until her sister was asleep tonight and read it in the bathroom. Jennifer usually hid things under her mattress and Maggie was very good at getting them and putting them back so that Jen never suspected anything.

It had been quite a day, Maggie thought, and it wasn't over yet.

# THE NOTEBOOK (12)

**S**o Sam – do you think the killing had anything to do with Brady or was it just about the necklace?

If Brady's still CIA I don't see how. It's got to be the necklace – Probably just murder and theft.

*Okay, then who was it – the victim, I mean?*

No idea. You were right about wig and not real Señorita.

*Could have been man – with the wig and padded to look like a woman? Sundress only cut low in back.*

Nope. You looked at necklace – did you see Adam's apple above?

*Dunno. Too busy looking at necklace. Must have been worth fortune. Why would Secret Agent be wearing fortune in diamonds?*

Some kind of money transfer? No foreign funds to declare? Payment for something illegal? Dunno?

*Whatever. Okay what about body? Why dump it there?*

Right. Very dramatic. Lots of attention. Why?

*Distraction? Gives time for getaway?*

Okay. Somebody kills or knocks out fake señorita – gets diamonds – brings body to moat – takes off shoes –

[Zig zag line indicating interruption as notebook snatched away]

*SHOES? What about shoes?*

Shoes lying by railing – you practically stood on one.

So as I was saying before you rudely snatched book away – takes off shoes and throws body in moat. AND NOBODY NOTICES!!!

*We were at buffet.*

Whole world wasn't at buffet!

[Interruption as Grandmother speaks]

*You took picture of body in moat? Where's camera – let's look!*

Put camera in bottom of backpack in case Police were checking everyone on way out. Backpack now in trunk. Look later.

*Okay. Body in moat – Wig caught on rock – Funny haircut – Body looked wrong.*

Think so? Maybe just way it landed. Neck twisted.

*Would there be blood if killed earlier?*

Good point. Don't know. Maybe.

*Don't think it was blood.*

WHAT???

*Looked like red scarf or hanky under head.*

I didn't see that.

*I look binoculars, you look camera lens. Didn't look like blood to me. Too even. Don't know – just seemed wrong.*

Whole thing is WRONG. We'll see if picture shows any better.

*Grand's right. BE CAREFUL!*

You too!

The minute he was in his room, Sam locked the door and removed everything from his backpack. Most of it he dumped in his top dresser drawer. Carefully he removed the memory stick from his camera and placed it in the printer attachment.

He didn't have much time. And most of the pictures were ones he'd snapped before he saw the body. He did several prints of that though, enlarging as much as he could and then getting the main long shot. Studying the enlargement of the head, he wondered if Jennifer was right. What he'd thought was blood to begin with didn't look much like it now. Too smooth. Too something else he couldn't quite identify.

Carefully he tucked the prints into his notebook and put them and the camera back in his backpack, swung it onto his shoulder and left.

They were all waiting for him in Mrs. Arnold's room. Maggie was brandishing a magnifying glass. He wondered where she'd picked that up. There was no telling with Maggie – she might just have brought one along.

"Okay!" Jennifer was bouncing with impatience. "Hand 'em over!"

Sam resisted the temptation to fumble with the snap on his backpack just to bug her. Still, it took him a bit of time to dig out the notebook.

"Just a minute!" he said, as Jennifer snatched the prints out of his hands.

They moved the table lamp closer, but the room was dark and the light bulb seemed to be very dim.

"I've got one of those disposable flashlights in my room," Maggie was heading for the door as she spoke. "Back in a jiff...."

The door shut behind her and opened again almost immediately.

"That was a mighty short jiff," Jennifer said, without looking away from the prints.

Sam did look. Maggie had obviously turned back immediately and stood white-faced in the doorway.

"Sam," she said, "that's your room next to ours, isn't it?"

Sam nodded. She had everyone's attention now. She closed the door softly behind her.

"Somebody was going in...I just saw a man's back and then the door closed."

Sam had never seen Grand move so quickly. She had the door open and was looking down the hall. "Sam!" she said as she turned back. "What did you leave behind?"

Sam felt sick. He knew instantly what she meant, and he couldn't believe he'd been so dumb. "The printer," he said, "and it's got the memory stick with the pictures on it...."

There wasn't time to say more. He was rushing down the hall with Mrs. Arnold, his key in his hand. But he didn't have time to use it. The door swung open and a man shoved him aside. He hit the floor hard.

He was down, but it just gave him a better chance to see what happened next. A foot in a Dr. Scholl's sandal came out right before Sam's eyes and the man went down. The small Canon printer slid out of his hands. He was up in a moment, but not fast enough. Jennifer had swooped in, grabbed the printer and run into Grand's room. Sam could hear the door slam and the click of the lock. The man paused for a moment outside the door, then just kept running. He leapt over the balcony railing and disappeared.

"We're on the second floor!" Maggie ran over to look down. She stared a moment as Sam picked himself up and Mrs. Arnold picked up her sandal that had been knocked off. "Now," Maggie said as she came to meet them, "we've got a moustached Mexican with a little woolen hat *and* a limp to watch out for! Jennifer!" she called knocking on the door. "It's safe now! You can let us in!"

Obviously Maggie hadn't been too affected by the excitement, Sam thought. She was enjoying this very much.

Her grandmother, on the other hand, was looking extremely concerned. Grim. Inside the room she carefully locked the door, then went to the bathroom, checking windows and closets.

By the time she came back to them, Jennifer and Maggie had lost their triumphant looks and were beginning to look nervous. Sam just rubbed his knee. Mexican tiles were beautiful but painfully hard.

"I think we're going to have to skip our tour of Chichen Itza for now," Mrs. Arnold said bitterly, "and go straight on to Uxmal." She didn't wait for comment. "In fact," she sighed, "it might be wise to pack up and go tonight, except for the fact that we're probably safer here than driving all that way in the dark."

"Surely," Maggie protested, "he won't try again?"

"He knows we've seen him," put in Jennifer.

"Maybe we should call the police or tell the hotel, at least?" Sam added.

"I'm not sure telling the hotel is a good idea Sam. He must have had a key to be able to get into your room. That means we'd be dealing with some sort of conspiracy." She smiled at them reassuringly now. "A very small conspiracy... he'd just have to know one of the maids or bellmen and persuade them to lend him a passkey."

"And the police wouldn't do anything probably," Jennifer put in. "After all he didn't steal anything, did he?" She held out the printer to Sam.

It hadn't dawned on him until now that Señor Woolen Hat might have been smart enough to take the memory stick out and put it in his pocket. "No," he said, feeling relieved. "He didn't get away with anything."

"Right," said Maggie. "And the police might want to know why Sam's pictures were so important...and then we'd have to go into the dead señorita stuff at Xcaret."

"And speaking of Sam's pictures..." Mrs. Arnold said, "I wonder how our friend in the woollen hat knew about them. Did anyone see him at Xcaret?"

Three puzzled faces, and three people shook their heads.

"No," said Jennifer. "The last time we saw him was at Coba."

"But there were two people there who'd been at Coba."

"Brady and that Greek Tycoon!" Maggie looked perplexed. "One of them must have some kind of connection with the man in the woolen hat!"

"Or with someone who does..." Grand said thoughtfully. She was silent for a moment as the others waited expectantly, but when she finally spoke it was to change the subject. "Where were we when all of this began?"

"I was getting a flashlight." Maggie was already at the door.

"Not alone!" Sam hurried after her. "I don't think any of us should venture out alone."

"Very wise, Sam." The girls grandmother laughed. "Or should I say, Sam*wise* Gamgee!"

In the hall, Maggie laughed too. "She'll never be able to give that old nickname a rest, you know. You'd better be prepared to be called Sam Gamgee for a long time!"

Sam watched Maggie unlock the door to her and Jennifer's room. He didn't really mind the tease. And, if it had been Mrs. Arnold's intention to take their minds off their worries, it had worked.

It was easy to see which side of the room had been chosen by each twin. Maggie's suitcase sat open on the luggage stand by her bed. It took her only a moment to find the flashlight. Had they had to search for anything in the chaos that belonged to Jennifer it could have taken hours, though the contents of her suitcase were in plain sight – dumped, heaped and strewn all over the other bed and the floor beyond.

Studying the pictures with the flashlight and magnifying glass took them awhile. In the end they were no further along. The "blood" did look unnatural, but Sam had never seen blood around a dead body, so how could he really tell?

Finally, Mrs. Arnold put the pictures down with a sigh. "Well, my dears, we've been doing this for an hour and don't seem to be any further along...and I, for one, am famished. What do you say we get ourselves to the restaurant before they close." She smiled at Sam, "I think that all your camera and printing equipment fits nicely in your backpack, doesn't it Sam?"

Sam nodded and began to pack everything. Since someone had passkeys and access to the rooms, from now on they'd be carrying anything important.

Maggie was carefully gathering the prints to go in Sam's notebook when she let out a little squawk. "Look, Sam!" she said, pointing, "You must have been taking a shot of that cayman in the moat earlier on...see?" She grabbed the magnifying glass. "There's something red further on...it's...it *is*...there's a red scarf! Isn't that about where the body ended up later on?"

There was a scuffle as everyone tried to look at the picture at once.

"When did you take that one, Sam?" asked Mrs. Arnold.

Sam thought about it. "It was around the time that Maggie was speculating on somebody invisible being able to get by that 'gator." The more he thought about it the more sure he was. "Before we saw Brady and the señorita."

"So..." Maggie said softly. "Someone dropped that scarf down there...."

"And later," Jennifer blurted, "dropped the body on top?" Everyone looked confused.

"I wonder..." said Grand softly, "it seems too remarkable to have been a coincidence. Someone evidently had planned ahead." She turned away, talking to herself as she picked up her purse and went to the door. "Somebody who knew the señorita and Brady would be there...with the necklace." She shook her head. "They planned a switch, I wonder why?"

Curiouser and curiouser, Sam thought as they went to dinner.

Jennifer hadn't expected to be hungry. The excitement with the discovery of Señor Woolen Hat as Sam had begun to call him, made her think she couldn't eat. Especially now that she had the business of the red scarf to think about. Had someone actually planned the whole thing so far as to drop a scarf where they were going to throw an already dead body so that the red would look like blood?

"Of course," said Maggie. "It could have been that someone just accidently dropped the scarf earlier in the day...."

Sometimes, Jennifer thought, you'd think Maggie was reading my mind. Usually when that happened it annoyed her. This time she didn't care.

"It could be," Sam said doubtfully, "but as your grandmother said there'd be a couple of strange coincidences going on...for the body to land right there."

"But how would anyone be able to drop the body that accurately anyway," Jennifer put in, "so that it would land right on top of the scarf? They'd be taking quite a risk."

She looked at her grandmother expectantly. Why wasn't Grand getting in on the conversation? She'd done nothing but look around since they were seated at their table.

Jennifer looked too. The restaurant was nearly empty. And none of the other diners looked familiar. Something had happened though. The delicious aromas coming from the kitchen made her realize that she was famished. After all, she hadn't eaten much of her lunch.

She grabbed the menu the waiter had placed in front of her. "Too bad it's not a buffet," she said. "I don't know what half this stuff is."

Maggie laughed. "Right! That doesn't stop you at a buffet...you just take everything!"

Jennifer decided to let Maggie get away with that. "Sure, but at least I can see what I'm getting."

"Try the Chicken Yucataneca." Grand had stopped staring about the room and settled in to read the menu. "It may not be the same as the Colonel's, but I think you'll like the herbs and spices they use."

"I'm just going to have the *Sopa de Lima*," Maggie said, putting down her menu. "If it's as good as what we had in Cancun, it will be just fine. And I'm not all that hungry."

Jennifer remembered that Maggie, at least, had managed to finish her lunch before the screaming started.

"Besides," Maggie said looking cheerful. "If I just have soup I'll have room for dessert."

"Planning is everything, right Maggie?" laughed Sam.

Grand was looking pleased. "I must say that if I'm ever in a tight spot and want to have people around me who know how to dispel the tension...I'd choose you three every time."

Jennifer was glad to see Grand looking more relaxed. Maybe she'd change her mind about leaving first thing in the morning and they'd get to check out Chichen Itza after all.

The chicken was good, with its crispy, spicy crust. She liked spicy food anyway and even the rice it came with had bits of chili peppers. Combined with the yellow corn it was a very attractive meal. Jennifer was beginning to feel much better. So much so that she decided now was a very good time to give the spell another try.

"Excuse me," she said getting up from the table. "I'll just use that restroom we passed as we came into the restaurant." It was a lie. She had no intention of doing so. She'd head into the little gift shop and dawdle about waiting to become invisible.

Unfortunately for Jennifer, Maggie excused herself too. "You probably shouldn't go alone, Jen." She turned to Grand, "Remember? We're going to do things in twos."

Trust Maggie to louse things up, Jennifer thought. She didn't say anything until they were far enough away from their table that Grand couldn't overhear. "Thanks, Maggie!" she hissed. "You've messed things up once again! That was a lie to see if I could become invisible. I had no intention of going to the can!"

Instead of apologizing, as Jennifer expected, it was Maggie's turn to be indignant. "So what would you have done? Wandered about the hotel? Gone up to the room? What if Señor Woolen Hat was there? He wouldn't have run from one person...you could have been the one thrown over the railing this time!"

They were in the restroom now – so much for a lie to become invisible, Jennifer thought. She checked for feet under all the cubicles. Nobody there. She decided just to perch on the counter by the sink and wait for Maggie. Maybe if she didn't actually *use* the toilet the spell would work. She didn't hold out much hope though. Sitting there gave her time to think about Maggie's last remark.

"You think it was Señor Woolen Hat who murdered the pseudo señorita?" The possibility hadn't occurred to her before. "We didn't see him at Xcaret, just the other day at Coba."

"That's true," Maggie admitted. "I checked all of Sam's photos, just in case the man showed up in the background, and he didn't."

Good old Muggins, Jennifer thought. Thorough. She hadn't thought to do that.

"We should," Maggie added, "probably sit down and go through all the pictures he's taken since we arrived, in case there are people who turn up more than once."

"Tomorrow!" Jennifer said, leaping down from the counter as Maggie came to wash her hands. "We can do it in the car on the way to Uxmal. The light will be better...and nobody can interrupt us."

"I wish we weren't going to miss touring Chichen Itza though," Maggie said wistfully as they headed back to the restaurant.

Jennifer was careful to look down the corridor to the hotel rooms. Nobody there except a waiter pushing a cart with trays on it.

There was someone seated at the table next to theirs when they got back. She supposed that was why Sam was looking like a stormcloud.

When Sam first saw the white hat coming into the restaurant he couldn't believe it. Surely it wasn't the Greek Tycoon again – wouldn't the man have gone back to his yacht? What was he doing here?

Mrs. Arnold didn't seem concerned. She too was watching the man enter the restaurant and wait for the waiter to seat him.

"I see, we weren't the only ones at Xcaret who had Chichen Itza scheduled for the next stop," she said sipping her water.

"Maybe he followed us..." Sam couldn't believe this was a coincidence. He remembered the black limousine Jennifer told him had been behind them when they left Xcaret. Though he had to admit they'd watched very carefully and there'd been no sign of it once they'd left the highway at Tulum.

The man was shaking his head as the waiter pointed to a table. In an almost deserted restaurant it appeared he was insisting that he have the table next to them. The waiter was leading him this way. The nerve!

"Good evening, Señora," he said, removing his hat and bowing to Mrs. Arnold.

Sam was pleased that she didn't reply, even though she did acknowledge the bow by nodding graciously as she had that afternoon at the restaurant at Xcaret.

He would love to pin a murder on this guy, but he had to admit that the man had an alibi – he'd been in the restaurant when they had. No! Wait a minute! Sam thought back to lunch. The Greek Tycoon hadn't been there until they came back from the buffet. He could have been dumping the so-called señorita in the moat while they were getting their food.

Sam stared at the man defiantly – a scenario worthy of Jennifer was playing out in his mind. The señorita had been one of the many women in the Greek playboy's life. He'd probably given her the diamonds early in their affair. And, having seen her with Brady, he'd killed her in a fit of jealous rage, removed the necklace and dumped her in the moat on his way to lunch. But if the fake señorita had already killed the one who'd been with Brady and taken the diamonds and his theory about the "romance" was true it didn't make sense. Surely the Greek playbody wouldn't have been fooled by some guy in a wig dressed as a woman. Two things were definite – Brady's lady had disappeared and someone dressed to look like her was dead.

He was so busy with this idea that it wasn't until Jennifer jabbed him in the ribs that he realized the girls were back from the restroom.

He could see that Jennifer was bursting with curiosity, but she was going to have to hold it until later. The tables were too close for them to safely talk about anything important. And they couldn't pass notes with Grand and Maggie sitting there. He hoped since they had all finished eating they would go back to the room. It would serve the Greek Playboy right if he was left sitting alone.

"I think I'll have dessert now," Maggie said. She seemed blissfully unaware that both Jennifer and Sam were staring at her shaking their heads.

Her grandmother was studying the menu. "There's not much choice, several different kinds of *el helado*...that's ice cream. Oh you might see if the waiter would bring you a selection of *el pastel*...that's cake." She studied the menu.

"I'll take a chance," said Maggie as the waiter arrived. "*El pastel,*" she said, "*por favor.*"

Jennifer rolled her eyes at Sam. They were obviously stuck here for another course. He shrugged philosophically.

"I'll have the *helado de vainilla.*" He figured that if Mexican vanilla was so famous, their vanilla ice cream should be something special. "Please." He didn't look at Jennifer, she'd be rolling her eyes again at his attempt at Spanish, but Maggie was smiling at him approvingly. You win some, you lose some, and sometimes you just break even, he thought.

"I'll have chocolate ice cream," Jennifer said.

"And I," said Mrs. Arnold, "will have *el flan.*"

"What's that?" Maggie asked after the waiter had departed.

"Crême caramel," laughed her grandmother. "And you know how that can differ from restaurant to restaurant at home. There's no telling what it will be like here!"

Sam watched as the waiter took the Greek playboy's order. He was still annoyed at the man for sitting so close to them. Once or twice it seemed as if the man was going to lean over and speak to Grand, but each time Sam would glare at him and he'd settle back in his chair.

Finally they'd finished. *"La cuenta, por favor,"* Mrs. Arnold said to the waiter.

The man just smiled and nodded toward the next table. "The Señor has asked that he might be permitted to cover the cost of your meal, Señora!"

Sam was indignant, but Mrs. Arnold just smiled and nodded and led them out of the restaurant. Now the rest of the evening would be spent with Jennifer and Maggie going on about this billionaire's generosity to their grandmother and he wouldn't get a chance to tell Jennifer of his suspicions about the man. Since they'd left the restaurant he'd added a few details. Was Señor Woolen Hat in any way connected to the Greek Playboy? Perhaps that launch in Cancun had been on its way out to the yacht – what was the name of it? The Agamemnon?

They walked Sam back to his room, went in to check that there was no one there. Mrs. Arnold even checked in the big cabinet where the TV was before she and the girls left. "Be sure to put the chain on your door, Sam." It was a reminder he didn't need.

He decided that he'd sleep with his backpack under the pillow next to him with the strap hooked around his wrist just in case. It wasn't going to be a good night.

Jennifer hadn't been too happy when Maggie made her slide the heavy chest of drawers over in front of their door. Fortunately it went smoothly along the tiles – they'd never have been able to lift it. Now it would take some sort of battering ram to get into their room.

Grand had insisted in coming in and checking their bathroom, under the bed and the TV cabinet too, although Maggie couldn't imagine anybody being able to squeeze in there. Some tiny Mexican contortionist, perhaps? Then they'd gone to Grand's room and checked everything there. After that she'd watched from her doorway as Maggie and Jennifer went back to their own room. No question about it, Grand had the wind up about the attempted theft of Sam's printer and pictures.

And she'd refused to talk about that Skopakos guy. Just accepted that it was all right for him to suddenly show up and buy their dinners. Even Jennifer's formidable questioning once they got to the room hadn't produced anything more than a mysterious smile from Grand. As Sam, always quoting Alice in Wonderland, would say, curiouser and curiouser.

**T**o Maggie's relief nothing happened during the night. No midnight prowlers, no faces at the window – Jennifer was obviously disappointed. It took them quite a while to push the chest of drawers back when Grand knocked on their door at seven o'clock. Maggie wasn't sure what dark wood the Mexican furniture was made from, but it weighed a ton. They must have had adrenalin working for them the night before to have moved it at all.

Breakfast was uneventful. Everyone ordered the *huevos rancheros*, which Grand recommended and which turned out to be simply fried eggs on a tortilla covered with a sort of salsa sauce. There was no sign of the Greek Tycoon – whom Maggie had expected to see, or of Señor Woolen Hat – whom she hadn't.

"We'll check out right away. Everyone all look in all the drawers and shelves in case you missed packing anything," she said as she left them at the doors to their rooms.

"Looks like Grand really meant it when she said we were leaving early," Jennifer said, cramming things into her suitcase.

"Right," said Maggie sadly, "I really wanted to see Chichen Itza. It's the most famous place in the Yucatan."

She felt better later, sitting in the backseat of the car with Sam when he said that his grandfather had told him that it was not nearly as old a site as Uxmal. "Half the area around the pyramid they call the Castle, Grandad said, is Toltec!"

Good to know, Maggie thought. She had picked up a guide book for Chichen Itza as well as one for Uxmal in the hotel gift shop in Cancun and she pulled it out of her backpack and began to read.

"Hey, this is interesting! Did you know that the Aztec god Quetzalcoatl – which for your information means 'feathered serpent' – was called Kukulcan by the Mayas?"

"Wasn't that the name of the boulevard our hotel was on in Cancun?" Sam asked.

Jennifer nodded. "And Carlos & Charlie's restaurant. Remember the great enchiladas we had that first night?"

Trust Jennifer to remember the food.

"It says," Maggie said reading, "Kukulcan was the most important divinity in Chichen Itza, reigning side by side with Chac, the Mayan god of rain."

"Easy to understand why the god of rain would be important. People wondered why the Mayans would leave their cities from time to time, but recent studies by some scientist in Sweden of the rings of trees indicated that there was a world-wide drought each time the cities were abandoned." Sam informed them. "Studying the rings of trees is called Dendrology...it's amazing what can be learned about the effects of climate from the annual growth rings in the trees. I saw it on the Learning Channel." He paused and thought a bit. "Or maybe the scientist studied trees in Sweden and he was from somewhere else..."

"Always good to get the facts, Sam!" Jennifer said sarcastically.

"Oh, and Jennifer," added Maggie, "it seems that all those jaguars on the Mayan sites were added by the Olmecs."

"Another 'ec' and I'll be sick," said Jennifer dramatically making the gagging sign by sticking her finger in her mouth. "Eck!"

Maggie gave her a look of disgust. It would be such fun travelling with just Sam and Grand, she thought. A person might actually learn something. She decided a little revenge was in order.

"Oh Jennifer," she said sweetly. "Did you check to see if you'd left anything in the bathroom, the way Grand asked you to?"

Maggie knew very well Jen hadn't. She'd gone in and gathered up Jennifer's shampoo, toothpaste and toothbrush after her sister had left dragging her bursting suitcase and backpack down to the checkout desk.

Jennifer glared. "Thank you so much for reminding me now, Maggie. Of course I did!"

Maggie didn't say a word. She'd make Jennifer beg for that toothbrush later.

"**H**ow come we haven't come to the highway yet?" Sam asked. "Aren't we taking the Toll Road to Merida?"

Grand shook her head. "It's shorter going across country. And I thought the drive through these little villages and towns would be interesting."

Maggie thought Grand looked much more relaxed now that they were on the road. She obviously didn't expect any trouble.

Jennifer had picked up the *Cancun Tips* magazine and was studying the map in it. "It's not that much shorter Grand, and it winds up and down. And these roads are pretty narrow!" She threw the magazine back onto the dashboard.

"Oh, but look at the oriole's nests!" said Sam. "They're hanging from the phone lines or power lines or whatever they are."

"Look at that!" Jennifer said.

Maggie had taken her eyes off the Chichen Itza guide book at last. She looked to where Jennifer was pointing behind them. It looked to be the same ramshackle truck as yesterday or another one the same colour, and it was coming up behind them awfully fast. Was the driver actually going to try to pass them on this narrow road?

"Don't let him pass you, Grand!" Jennifer said.

"I'm afraid I don't have any choice," Grand said grimly. She braked and swerved just as the truck sped by, narrowly missing them.

"I wonder what the hurry is?" Sam said softly.

"Whatever it was, he seems to be slowing down now." Maggie was perplexed. "All that rush just to pass us and now he seems to be stopping and turning sideways in the road!" She was suddenly aware that they were far from any signs of civilization, other than the power lines and the truck that had now slowed down ahead of them. The road was, as Jennifer had pointed out, very narrow. "You know, that looks a lot like the old truck we met coming up from Tulum yesterday."

Grand looked serious, "I'm sure that there is more than one beat-up truck in Mexico, but I don't like the look of this."

"I don't feel well," Jennifer said suddenly.

Grand had braked the car as they watched to see what the vehicle ahead would do, now she was nearly stopped completely. "You're not carsick, are you?" She sounded concerned. "I've never known you to be carsick."

It was true. Maggie thought. Their mother said Jennifer had a cast-iron stomach. Nothing made her sick. Nothing except....

"Pass me that magazine with the map, Jennifer," Maggie leaned forward to look over the seat to where Jennifer sat.

The magazine rose from the dashboard and floated across to Maggie. Jennifer's hands had disappeared!

Obviously Jennifer didn't even realize what was happening. She disappeared bit by bit. She must have shut her eyes because she felt sick and didn't know.

"Ohhhh...." groaned Jennifer.

Maggie realized that Grand hadn't noticed what was happening as yet. Her eyes were on the road and the truck that was now turned crossways in the road ahead of them.

"If you're sick, dear girl, you could get out," she said. "I don't know what that driver ahead is up to anyway. It looks like he is trying to turn around."

It did look like that. The truck was now completely blocking the narrow road, nosed into the trees on one side. Grand had braked their car to a stop, waiting to see what would happen. Now the driver was getting out. At first Maggie thought he might be just going to check to see how much room he had to back up. Then she saw what he was wearing on his head. It couldn't be a coincidence.

"Oh, oh!" murmured Sam.

The man was walking back now. Grand had shifted the car into reverse and was trying to back away down the narrow road. Maggie craned her head to look behind. Amazingly there was another vehicle approaching. She doubted if that was a coincidence either. They would be caught in a vise. She looked to the front again. Señor Woolen Hat had pulled out a gun.

Grand kept on backing up. The man fired twice. Low. Their side of the car seemed to sink down as they stopped. He's shot out our tires, Maggie realized.

The man was moving toward them pointing the gun at Grand.

"Everyone out of the car!" he said.

Jennifer had disappeared completely by now. Maggie felt her flop half onto her as she slid over the seat into the back.

In the front seat Grand had opened her door. She turned to where Jennifer had been sitting. "Do as the man says," she said quietly. "Jennifer?" She sounded puzzled. Maggie realized that Grand had been so busy concentrating ahead that she didn't know Jennifer was gone. Quickly, Maggie opened her door, waited until she knew Jennifer had scrambled out, and then climbed slowly out herself. She felt Jennifer pat her on the back. Sam was sliding across the seat. Maggie held the door for him. He just looked at her and nodded.

"I'll take those," the man was pointing to the pile of photos on the back seat. Maggie knew Sam had kept them out of his backpack this morning. They were the ones they'd been planning to study as they drove to Uxmal. "And the camera!" Woolen Hat was waving the gun at Sam now. Reluctantly Sam began lifting the camera from around his neck.

Behind Grand, Maggie realized a broken branch was rising from beside the road and being dragged toward their assailant. If only Grand didn't see it and give things away.

Maggie thought Sam must have seen the stick too because he was moving very slowly, acting as if the camera strap was caught, trying to keep the man's attention.

Maggie hadn't realized that Grand was going to move too. At about the same time as the stick was raised to strike,

Grand moved with a karate chop toward the hand that held the gun. The blows landed almost at the same time. Woolen Hat lost his gun and went down from the blow to his head. Maggie dived for Sam just in case the gun fired. But Sam was ducking in her direction at the same time. They collapsed in a heap in the dirt.

That left only Grand standing when the black limousine pulled up.

By the time the man in the white hat stepped out of the back, Grand had retrieved the gun and was standing facing him.

**S**am hung onto Maggie as long as he could. He figured it was safer down there. He wasn't sure how good the girls' grandmother was with guns. He wouldn't mind a bit if she decided to take a potshot at the Greek Playboy now that she had the chance.

The heavy branch that had knocked out Señor Woolen Hat was leaning against their car. He was pretty sure that leaning with it was the invisible Jennifer. The spell couldn't have picked a better time to finally work for her.

"Ah, Señora!"

Sam had to hand it to the man. He was positively oozing charm and not a bit perturbed by the gun in Mrs. Arnold's hand.

"You seem to have encountered one of the famous *bandidos* they warn us tourists to look out for..."

Sam wasn't sure if now was a good time to stand up, but Maggie had moved over to lean against the car so he did too.

The girls' grandmother was still holding the gun. Sam was pleased to see she was pointing it steadily. He remembered her telling them in Istanbul that she'd been a karate class drop-out. Maybe she'd persisted in the gun-handling course – if she'd taken one.

The Greek Playboy seemed unfazed at having a gun trained on him. "It appears, Señora," he said gesturing toward their disabled car, "that your automobile has been incapacitated. Perhaps you would like to join me and my party to Uxmal. I believe you have reservations for tonight at the Hacienda Uxmal?"

Too much! Sam was seething. The nerve of the man! He's obviously checked into our every move.

"That's very kind of you." The gun didn't waver as she spoke. "Before we accept your offer, I would like to meet the other members of your party. Perhaps you could have them step out of your car?"

Sam had to hand it to Mrs. Arnold. She was being very cool. Her request was obviously clear enough. The back door of the limo opened and out stepped Mr. Brady.

That was a shocker, but even more amazing was the person who stepped out behind him. Sam could hear a gasp of shock from the invisible Jennifer, or maybe it was Maggie. He might even have done it himself.

She was not wearing a white sundress this time. She had on one of those embroidered flouncy Mexican dresses. Definitely not something to wear a diamond necklace with, but there it was – dazzling his eyes as the sunlight flashed from it. The diamonds were there, and so was the Señorita. Very much alive.

Sam's mind raced. It had been fake blood in the moat. Now their suspicions were confirmed. It had been a fake señorita as well. He felt Jennifer move away from the car beside him. He assumed she was going to get a better look.

Once again, he had to hand it to Mrs. Arnold. She must have been just as surprised as they were but she wasn't giving an inch. The gun remained steady.

"Those are all your passengers?" she said. "I assume you have a driver?"

The driver's door opened and a man in a chauffeur's cap stepped out. If seeing the dead Señorita resurrected was a surprise, here was a corpse from the past too. Sam gasped.

"Stavros?" Jennifer must have recognized him at the same time that Sam did. The bartender from the Stella Solaris, the cruise ship they'd been on in Greece, had been betrayed by a double agent and killed. Hadn't he?

Sam hoped the disembodied voice was still close enough that the Greek Playboy would assume it came from Maggie. Maggie was obviously thinking the same thing as she had moved forward to be closer to the man as she peered at the chauffeur. "It looks like Stavros, all right!"

"Unfortunately not!" his employer said sadly. "This is Stavros' brother Alekos." His eyes narrowed as he looked at Maggie. "And how did you know Stravros?"

Maggie looked worried, "He...he was a bartender on a cruise ship we were on last year...."

"That's right," Sam came to her rescue. "We heard that he'd died or disappeared or something..." He let his voice trail off as if he wasn't sure of the facts.

It seemed to satisfy the Greek Tycoon. The chauffeur nodded to Sam and stepped back to stand beside the car.

If my brain was a computer it would crash right now, Sam decided. Even if there was only one person resurrected from the dead it was more than enough to cope with. If the Señorita was still alive, diamonds and all, who was the person with the mannish haircut they'd seen dead at the bottom of the moat?

And more important, what was Brady doing with these people? Whose side was he on anyway?

**J**ennifer was confused. She circled around behind Grand just in case somebody made a false move and there was any shooting. She wanted to get close to the Señorita, who was standing beside the limousine distancing herself from Mr. Brady. If Grand did decide to shoot somebody, it would probably be one of the men, so she figured it would be fairly safe behind the Señorita. And she had to find something out.

She reached up and gave the Señorita's lush black hair a good tug. The young woman's head snapped back, and she looked around frightened and confused.

Not a wig, obviously. Everyone was looking at the young woman now. Grand had turned the gun her way, no doubt thinking that the Señorita had moved in preparation to do something. Had Brady begun to reach inside his jacket too?

Jennifer decided it would be wise to get out of range. The back door of the limo was still open. She slipped inside. She'd be out of sight and it wouldn't hurt to check around before everyone climbed back in.

It wasn't until she was inside that she realized Grand probably thought she was still back at the car, armed with the trusty branch she'd used to club Woolen Hat. Not good! She'd better get back there as quickly as possible.

Too late! As Jennifer bent over and began to climb out of the car the chauffeur slammed the back door, catching her on the top of the head. She fell backwards. Down but not out. Not quite. She wasn't exactly seeing stars, but her head felt as if it would explode.

It took all her strength to crawl onto one of the side seats before she collapsed completely.

**M**aggie was too amazed by the events unfolding before her to give much thought to what Jennifer was doing just now. The Señorita was obviously very much alive. She'd puzzle about that later. Right now she couldn't imagine what on earth Mr. Brady was doing hanging around with a mysterious Greek billionaire. If the man hadn't been mysterious before he certainly was now. What on earth could be the connection? Was the fact that he was employing the brother of a murdered secret agent significant?

She stayed close by Sam at a safe distance from where Grand still held the gun trained on the people from the limousine. She noticed that Sam had picked up the branch that had fallen on the ground beside their car. He was, she realized, keeping an eye on Señor Woolen Hat, who still lay motionless on the ground nearby. Good grief, she thought, I hope Jennifer didn't kill him!

She moved over to peer at him, just in case.

"Don't get too close, Maggie!" Grand commanded. "We don't want him coming to and grabbing you."

Maggie backed quickly away. Grand was certainly keeping an eye on everyone.

"And thank you, Sam," Grand said nodding his way. "Feel free to bash our woolen-capped friend with the branch again, if he stirs. I'd prefer he didn't know how we left when he comes to."

"Right!" said Sam.

"Mr. Brady," Grand's voice was stern. "It would be very nice if you'd explain exactly what your position is just now." She softened a little. "That is, if you can safely do so."

That's interesting, thought Maggie, she's giving him a chance to keep his cover. So Grand still trusts him. She caught a look from Sam. Obviously he was trying to figure it out too.

Brady glanced at the Señorita and paused for only a moment before replying. "This young lady claims to be Conchita de Lapiz and she is accompanying me until her 'friends' arrive. She tells me that she is merely the innocent transporter of the lovely jewels you see her wearing. Soon, she tells me, they will be turned over. I assume it is payment for an important commodity that interests me very much."

Brady had moved forward now. He was still a respectful distance from Grand and them but now he was a bit in front of the man in the white hat.

"If you must know," he continued, blinking his eyes rapidly, "I am an agent for the DEA, on assignment in Mexico." He nodded to Grand. "I believe you will be perfectly safe accepting Mr. Skopakos' kind offer." He gestured toward the man lying on the ground. "It might be wise to leave before that man comes to."

Grand nodded and turned to Maggie and Sam. "I think we'll have to risk it," she said quietly. "We certainly can't remain here." Briskly she walked to the car and removed her purse.

"We will accept your kind offer, Mr. Skopakos. Perhaps your driver would be good enough to help move our luggage into your car?" She turned, "When you finish gathering up your photographs, Sam, would you mind helping?"

I hope she's not going to abandon that gun, Maggie thought. She was relieved to see Grand slip it into her handbag. Maggie went to grab her and Jennifer's backpacks. She hoped the others would just assume that the third backpack belonged to Grand. The next thing she'd have to do would be get into the limo and be sure there was a place for Jennifer to sit.

"Just a minute," Grand called to Mr. Brady as he and the Señorita were about to re-enter the limo. "Would you mind waiting and letting the youngsters get in first?"

She didn't bother to explain, but the others waited as Maggie went back, giving Grand a grateful look as she did.

Where was Jennifer anyway, she wondered? She opened the door and pretended to drop something so that she bent down away from the door, giving Jennifer time to slip by. Strange? She was pretty sure her sister would have had to at least touch if not bump her on the way in but she hadn't felt anything. Where was she? Maggie could only hope that Jennifer would be able to get in on Sam's side.

Her mind was racing anyway. So much new information. Brady said he was DEA. Was that his cover story or had he really switched from CIA to the Drug Enforcement Agency to work here in Mexico? Did that sort of thing happen?

She moved in to sit on one of the seats along the side and nearly sat on someone. Jennifer! So that's where she was. So far Brady and the Señorita were still standing waiting for Sam to finish helping the chauffeur – what was Stravros' brother's name? Al– something? She was alone with Jennifer. She decided to take a chance.

"Good thing you decided to sit on the side opposite the bar, Jen..." she whispered. "In case one of them decides to have a drink."

There was no reply.

"Jennifer?" She leaned against her sister. Jennifer seemed to be flopped against the back of the seat ahead. Maggie was grateful that the others wouldn't be able to see through the tinted windows, and though the rear door was still open, Brady and the Señorita were too far away to see inside. She grabbed Jennifer by the shoulder and pulled her towards her. To Maggie's horror, her sister fell against her – a dead weight.

"Jennifer!" It took all of Maggie's determination not to scream the word.

Surely using the spell again after so long couldn't have killed her twin. What had happened to Jennifer?

Frantically, Maggie felt for Jennifer's arm. How do you feel for a pulse when you can't find the wrist? To her relief she heard her sister take a breath. She was alive at least.

Sam doubted the wisdom of accepting a ride with the Greek Playboy – he didn't trust him for a minute. He still thought there might be a connection between him and the man who'd shot out their tires. The arrival of the sleek black limousine at that precise moment was just too convenient to be coincidence.

Brady's involvement, he thought as he handed another suitcase to the driver to stow in the limo's trunk, really puzzled him too.

Any reading Sam had done about the CIA seemed to emphasize the jealousy between it and the FBI and other agencies. He wondered if the Drug Enforcement Agency could be any different. Maybe, he thought, that was just Brady's cover story. But then, what was the connection with the Señorita's diamonds? It did make sense that the necklace – probably worth a million or two – could be payment for a shipment of drugs. But wouldn't the delivery need to be made in the United States? There was the whole Gulf of Mexico between the Yucatan peninsula and the nearest of the southern states.

Of course, if you had a fast motor launch, or better yet a yacht that was constantly cruising through International waters, who would stop you?

Alekos interrupted Sam's speculations. "Do you want me to put your backpack in with the young lady's?"

Sam looked to where the driver was pointing in the trunk. Maggie and Jennifer's backpacks lay amongst the luggage.

No way! he thought. "No thank you," he said politely. "I'll just keep it with me."

Actually, he thought, judging by his Greek accent, and the fact that he looks so much like Stavros, if I were going to trust anybody right now this Alekos might just be the man.

He watched as his man walked over to the truck that was blocking the roadway and began to carefully back it off into the bushes. It looked to Sam as if the old truck was so tangled in the undergrowth now that it would take a lot of chopping and pushing to extricate it. There was, however, just enough room for their limo to get by, although not without a severe scratching from the branches on the other side of the road. Sam assumed billionaires didn't care about such things. He knew he should get into the car now, but he wanted to see what became of Woolen Hat. They couldn't very well leave him lying in the middle of the road.

Obviously, that wasn't the intention. Alekos lifted him up and sat him in the driver's seat of the old truck. If you came upon the scene later you'd just think he was asleep. He'd regain consciousness and wonder where he was for a minute. As Sam climbed into the back seat, he wondered just how long it would be before that happened. Jennifer certainly packed a wallop.

He went to sit beside Maggie, but she shook her head and pointed to the seat across from her beside the bar. He could see her frantically trying to signal some information about the seat beside her – obviously where Jennifer was sitting. He nodded. Not a problem.

But Maggie seemed to think it was. "Sam!" she sounded almost in tears. But that was all she got to say. The Señorita and Brady were climbing into the back seat.

Sam settled back. He was sorry to see that Maggie was taking things so hard. It was true they probably were still in danger, especially if his suspicions about the Greek Tycoon were correct. At least he hadn't murdered the Señorita. But now that he thought about it *somebody* had murdered someone at Xcaret.

The chauffeur had come around and opened the back door on the other side. He was politely waiting for Mrs. Arnold and his employer to get in, but there seemed to be a disagreement.

"I really would prefer to sit up front with the driver," she said.

"No! No! Dear lady," he was saying, "in case there is further trouble on the road, it would be best if I did so. You can then sit in the back and make sure all is well with our passengers." Sam saw him nod toward her purse, as if to indicate that she might wish to use the gun again.

For a moment it looked as if she would protest more, but then Sam saw her climb into the car and sit in a corner of the back seat, distancing herself from the Señorita and Brady.

As soon as they were settled, the window separating the front seat was rolled down.

To Sam's annoyance it appeared that they weren't rid of the Greek Playboy after all.

"Señora Arnold is it?" Did the man never run out of charm? Sam wondered. "Now that we have a moment to speak, I must ask...did you not have *two* young ladies travelling with you?"

Of course, Sam realized, everyone knew about Jennifer. Even Mr. Brady.

Mrs. Arnold seemed unfazed. "Poor Jennifer," she said, "wasn't feeling up to the trip today so she stayed behind with a friend of mine at the hotel. We'll pick her up on our return tomorrow."

"Oh," said Skopakos smoothly. "I was told that someone saw her checking out of the hotel and leaving with you."

"No!" Maggie interrupted, her voice almost hysterical. "She's very sick...can't move...can't move at all!" Maggie was looking at her grandmother as she spoke.

Strange, thought Sam. Maggie certainly seems upset.

Skopakos seemed startled by the vehemence of Maggie's interruption but he obviously decided to let the matter drop. Mrs. Arnold, however was definitely looking worried now.

Sam settled back. His back was to the window on his side but he could see quite well out of the window across from him. He knew the seat facing him was not really empty. He got a kick out of the idea that he was actually looking through Jennifer. For a moment he stared, trying to imagine her sitting there facing him. Probably, because he was staring she'd be making faces at him now – sticking out her tongue or something. He had to control the urge to grin. And to make a face back. After all, the Greek Playboy was still turned looking into the back seat and could see him quite clearly.

He continued to stare. It was then that he noticed some-thing on the back of the seat Jennifer was on. A stain. Something red. And the stain was growing.

Sam felt a shiver go up his spine as he realized what it was. Blood. Jennifer was bleeding. As long as the blood was part of her it was invisible, but the minute it fell away he could see it.

He realized now that Maggie wasn't looking panic-stricken because she was afraid they were in danger. She knew something was wrong with Jennifer. And the only way they could help her would be to let all these people know about her invisibility. Could they do that?

Wordlessly he reached across and gave Maggie's hand a squeeze. He wanted to say something like, "It'll be all right, Maggie," or "Don't worry." But all he could do was let her know he'd figured it out.

The pain was awful. Jennifer opened her eyes, but the light hurt. Gradually, she remembered. She was in the car, the big black limousine belonging to that Greek Tycoon. She'd cracked her head on the door. She vaguely remembered Maggie beside her. If only it didn't hurt so much. Without meaning to, she moaned softly.

Almost immediately, she heard Maggie echo the sound.

She could hear concern in Grand's voice. "Are you all right, my dear?"

Before Maggie could answer, the man in the front seat on the other side of Jennifer spoke too. "Is there a problem, young lady?"

It was a moment before Maggie answered. Jennifer was able to keep her eyes open. She could see Mr. Brady in the back seat beside the window, then the Señorita, and then at the other window was Grand, her hand inside the purse on her lap. The car was spacious enough that they weren't sitting very close to each other. Beside her on the seat was Maggie and facing them was Sam. Everyone, even the Greek Tycoon, who was peering through from the front seat into the back, was looking concerned. Everyone was looking at Maggie. Except Sam.

He's staring straight at me, thought Jennifer. Panic gripped her. Can he see me? Did being knocked out make me become visible again? She looked down. No. She could see nothing but the seat she sat on. But she shouldn't have moved her head like that. It almost made her pass out again.

"I...I...I'm okay...I think..." Maggie said.

"Not car sick, are you Dear?" Grand was leaning forward. "We could stop the car for a minute, if you like?"

Jennifer could feel Maggie hesitate. Getting out of the car would give Maggie a chance to talk to Grand in private. And if Jennifer could slip out too they could communicate what was wrong. The trouble was, Jennifer doubted very much that she could move to get out of the car just now. Maggie was just sitting there.

When they were little kids they used to play a game where they'd write words on each other's backs and try to guess. Now Jennifer reached over and printed an "N" and an "O" between Maggie's shoulders. For a moment she was afraid Maggie would be surprised into moving, but she wasn't.

"Nnno...No!" Maggie said. "Maybe later, but I think I'm all right for now."

Good old Muggins, Jennifer thought. She's left an opening so that we could get out later on. She patted her sister gently on the back. She was tempted to try to write. "T", "H", "A", "N", "K", "S" but feared Maggie would think it was something important that she couldn't figure out. Better leave it alone.

Obviously Maggie was already worried. Sam too. He was still staring at her. Or staring through her.

Neither of them, Jennifer decided was as worried as she herself was. Her head was clearing a bit, but she definitely wasn't about to move just yet.

Either they had turned around and were going back to Chichen Itza or the Greek Tycoon was driving them on to Uxmal. She hoped it was the latter. It was a long way and it would give her time to recuperate. She hoped.

They came to a village. The car braked and slowed, but still going over the *Topes* sent a jolt of pain through her head. Jennifer almost groaned again. In a way she wished she could pass out again. This was going to be a tough trip.

Brady had leaned forward to speak to Grand. Good, Jennifer thought. I need to be distracted from this headache.

"Mrs. Arnold?" he said, as if he was unsure of her name. "I think you deserve an explanation about Xcaret...the body there...I mean."

He's got everyone's attention now, Jennifer thought. Mine, anyway.

"The dead man was from a rival group, hoping to make contact with the people I'm pursuing. His pretense at being Conchita here was, unfortunately for him, discovered. Conchita's 'friends' chose to cancel both him and the exchange. Which is why," Brady looked at the Señorita, who was glaring straight ahead of her, "I am going to stay very, very close to Señorita de Lapiz for the next day or two."

I wonder, thought Jennifer. Perhaps the group Brady was talking about had meant simply to substitute their fake señorita for the real one. Just long enough to get the diamonds.

It was good having something to think about besides her pounding head. She reached up tentatively touching her tangled hair. It wasn't just tangled, it was matted. And wet. She was bleeding.

She'd expected a goose egg, but this was worse. She'd had her head down when the door slammed. Somehow the handle must have struck her and split her scalp. Don't panic, Jennifer, she told herself. Just because it's bleeding doesn't mean it's any worse. Didn't her mother say that head wounds bleed a lot? Jennifer was always bonking her head when she was a kid. This was no different. She hoped.

**M**aggie felt slightly, only slightly, better than she had when the limo had first set out. Then, she'd felt horribly frightened and alone. Jennifer unconscious, and she was the only one who knew about it.

Now, Jennifer was conscious, though evidently not well enough to leave the car. At least that was the way Maggie interpreted the "NO" on her back. And she wasn't the only one who was aware of Jennifer's condition. Sam obviously had figured it out and Grand seemed to know too.

She could feel some of the tension draining out of her as she settled back onto the seat. They were coming into a larger town now. Interesting. She could see the ruins of a huge church. Too bad the Guidebook was back in the car. Too bad they couldn't stop and go and see it. Too bad everything was not normal. She wished they could go back a few hours when the three of them were happily driving along with Grand. Everything safe, an ordinary tourist trip.

She looked back at the Señorita. Conchita de Lapiz, Brady had called her. Maggie admired the Señorita's dress. She'd examined a few of those lovely traditional dresses hanging in the markets in Cancun. Even been tempted to buy one. The cheaper ones were only two hundred pesos. A little more than $20 U.S.

Trouble was, those were not very impressive. A little machine embroidery. The one the Señorita was wearing was beautifully hand-embroidered. It must have taken someone weeks to do that, Maggie thought.

The Señorita was leaning forward now, looking out of the window. They were still driving through the town. Maggie glanced over. People were standing, staring at them. She supposed very few limousines had driven through this little place.

Her attention went back to the Señorita. For the first time the woman was showing some interest. No, more than that – emotion. Maggie wondered what the connection was. Obviously the town was familiar. Was this where she was to meet someone? Probably not. More likely, she knew someone here, had family or had even grown up here. That was it, Maggie was sure. The Señorita's beautiful brown eyes had tears in them. She caught Maggie watching her and looked down, lowering her lashes. A tear slid down her cheek and landed on the embroidery of her dress. Sitting next to her, Brady seemed oblivious.

"Señorita?"

Maggie was startled by the voice from the front seat. The Greek Tycoon had evidently been watching too.

"Would you like to stop?"

He's out of his mind! Maggie thought. Who knows what could happen. Of course the Señorita would like to stop. A perfect place to escape. If she came from this town, she'd have friends, brothers. How many would it take to overpower them? Three men, not counting Sam, and Grand with a gun. Maybe Brady had one too, but what good would that do in a town full of people? People who might be defending a native daughter. Their only advantage was the invisible Jennifer, but she was out of commission. The Greek Tycoon was obviously crazy.

"No..." said the Señorita. "*Gracias.*"

Maggie stared at her in amazement. The woman's eyes were still downcast, so she could read nothing in them. But the voice, Maggie thought, was full of regret.

She looked at Brady. She'd been right about the gun. His hand had gone inside his jacket and remained there. Señorita de Lapiz must have noticed that. Perhaps that was why she'd declined the offer. Maggie tried to read Brady's expression. There wasn't one. She wondered if he had been surprised or upset by the offer, but he was stone-faced. Perhaps they'd actually planned giving the Señorita that opportunity to see what she'd do.

They were out of the town now, passing fields of yucca growing in neat rows.

"They grow cactus here? Like a crop on their farms?" She blurted it without thinking.

"Yes," the Greek Tycoon responded, "I believe it is used in the making of liquor...Tequila? Mescal? Something like that. Interesting, is it not?" He was smiling at Maggie in a friendly way.

She almost smiled back. The man seemed friendly enough and he had been consistently helpful. The only thing that stopped her was the look on Sam's face. Señor Stormcloud again! No doubt about it, Sam had really taken a dislike to the Greek Tycoon. Maggie wondered how much of it was mistrust and how much had to do with the fact that Mr. Skopakas behaved so charmingly to Grand. She knew that Sam liked the idea of their grandparents being such good friends. She had to admit she did too. If Grand and Dr. Martell got together it might make for some interesting travel plans in the future. But she really thought the Greek billionaire was not a threat. If he wanted to follow them around paying for their meals and rescuing them with his limousine it was perfectly fine with her.

**S**am was relieved when they finally arrived at the Hacienda Uxmal. The limousine might have been dusty and a bit scratched but it was rather nice to pull up in style. No doorman in sight, but by the time they had climbed out and Alekos had begun to unload the luggage, a bellman or doorman or someone in uniform had appeared to help.

Sam took his time getting out of the car himself. He'd taken off his backpack and now he very carefully and slowly took off his camera and put it in the backpack. That way, he figured, Jennifer would have time to get out. If she could.

He was relieved when Maggie stuck her head back in the door and said, "Come on, Sam, we're waiting for you!" And then more softly, "Everybody's out!"

"Sorry," he said as he finally climbed out.

Maggie, he noticed, was standing leaning a bit. As if someone was pushing against her as she began to climb up the stone entrance steps. Oh, oh, he thought. Jennifer's still not in good shape. He'd been relieved to see that the little puddle of blood had stayed the same for most of the trip. Obviously, Jennifer wasn't bleeding anymore.

He moved up beside Maggie. If Jennifer was going to need help getting up the stairs he could provide some. He felt an arm go around his neck. So, he thought, she's holding onto Maggie like that on the other side. All they had to do was look as if they were walking together. Slowly. He hoped they wouldn't attract attention, but the others had gone ahead. Mrs. Arnold stood for a bit at the arched doorway looking anxiously their way, but when the Greek Playboy came solicitously back to see what was keeping her, she'd moved on across the foyer to the Registration Desk sign.

Good, Sam thought. The other men were still dealing with the luggage. He risked speaking. "Are you okay?" making it look as if he was talking to Maggie.

"A bit better now," Jennifer's voice replied.

He and Maggie spoke at once. "What happened?"

"Door slammed on head...knocked out...." Jennifer obviously wasn't going to waste energy speaking.

Sam was sure she was still groggy. At least judging by the weight she was leaning on them. Finally, they made it up the steps and into the hotel. To the right, ahead of them, was a little gift shop. A sign pointed to the Registration area to the left around the corner. As they came closer they could see the others. Mrs. Arnold was already being given keys.

"Let's just wait here," whispered Maggie. "Jen, you might have to walk past the others on your own, in case they notice Sam and I are walking funny. Can you do it?"

"Yeah, I guess so," Jennifer answered. Sam thought her voice sounded weak. He hoped she could.

"We'll catch up to you as soon as we're past the desk," Maggie whispered.

Mrs. Arnold came toward them, holding out the keys to Maggie. "Go ahead," she said, "I'll wait for the luggage." She looked concerned but didn't try to speak to Jennifer. "Your room is 106 and yours is 107, Sam." She dropped the key in his hand and turned back to the desk. She would keep the others distracted. Good, thought Sam.

They hadn't moved far when Jennifer's arm went around his neck again. It seemed weaker. He was afraid she wouldn't be able to hang on. He risked putting an arm around her waist to support her and felt Maggie do the same from her side. If the men coming in with the luggage noticed anything, it would just be that he and Maggie were trying to link arms. And not doing very well.

Once inside the room, they got Jennifer over to the bed.

"Can you talk?" Maggie demanded.

"Sure," said Jennifer sounding a bit more normal. "At least better than I can walk. Whew," she sighed and a head-shaped indentation appeared on the pillow. "It's good to lie down. But somebody get me a wet washcloth so I don't get blood on the pillow. I think I'm bleeding a bit."

Mrs. Arnold arrived with the luggage before Sam had a chance to explain that she'd bled a lot and the chauffeur would be wondering what had stained the car seat.

"I'm afraid that Sam and I will have to dine alone, Maggie," her grandmother said apologetically, after she'd been reassured that Jennifer's head wound was not serious. "We'll tell everyone that you still aren't feeling well and bring back enough food for the two of you. Besides, I don't like leaving Jennifer alone in case she had some concussion." She spoke toward the bed. "Try to keep awake...talk to Maggie."

Sam smiled as he went to his room – it shouldn't be hard to keep Jennifer talking; she really would have to be unconscious. He wasn't too thrilled with the idea of leaving the girls, though. He might even have tried to persuade Mrs. Arnold that he should stay too, but he was pretty sure the Greek Playboy would show up and he wasn't about to leave the girls' grandmother prey to his suave Mediterranean manners. The man should be watched. Too many people seemed to have fallen for his cheesy charm. Sam was determined not to be one of them.

To his amazement and relief, they were joined at dinner not only by the dreaded Greek but also by Mr. Brady and Señorita de Lapiz. Sam hardly noticed what he was eating – something *con pollo* that had a lot of rice involved – and he didn't eat much. He was too busy watching the others.

He couldn't for the life of him figure out what the connection between Brady and the Greek Playboy could be. Unless his guess about Skopakos being a drug smuggler had been true and he was the real quarry the so-called DEA agent was after. Then the Señorita was bait, not for some unknown gang but for the Greek Playboy. It made sense. And it was working. Skopakos was eating even less than Sam, he was so busy trying to charm the two women at the table.

Brady concentrated on his food, only pausing to check whenever someone new came into the dining room.

Mrs. Arnold seemed to be enjoying her meal, while graciously accepting the lavish compliments that came her way.

The Señorita looked more cheerful. She was smiling, sitting beside Sam and ignoring the Greek Playboy's blandishments.

"Are you enjoying your holiday, Señor?"

She's talking to me! Sam couldn't believe it. Those beautiful brown eyes were looking straight at him.

"Sam," he said, "not Señor...just Sam." He swallowed. No time to choke on his food. Thank goodness he hadn't just taken a mouthful.

"Sam?" She looked interested. "Is that short for Samuel? As in the Bible?"

Sam nodded. It was all he could do. The Señorita's attention – that beautiful face, those magnificent eyes – was focussed entirely on him. He felt as if there was a huge spotlight on him – nobody but him mattered.

"Should I call you Samuel? Or Sam?"

It was definitely a thousand watt smile. Sam realized he was nodding. Just sitting there, his head bobbing like one of those stupid car ornaments some people kept in their rear windows.

"You must call me Conchita...or just Chita." She leaned toward him a wave of intoxicating perfume enveloped him.

"Chita..." he gasped. At least he was speaking.

"It is a pleasant hotel," she said, "is it not?"

Sam restrained himself from saying that it had just become the most amazing hotel in the world. He was nodding again. Doggie-in-the-window. Say something, Sam. Anything.

"I...I hope you're all right," he blurted. "I mean...when we drove through that village...." Instantly he was sorry he'd mentioned it. Señorita de Lapiz's beautiful eyes welled up with tears. "Oh...oh, I'm so sorry...I didn't mean..." Why hadn't he just kept on doing the nodding head routine and kept quiet?

She smiled through the tears. "No, Señor Sam, it was just that the last time I was there someone died...someone I worked with...a very brave man." She glanced at Brady, then back to Sam. "It is why I am doing what I am doing now." It seemed even when she was sad her smile could dazzle him.

Everyone was standing up. It appeared the meal was over. Had they had dessert? Coffee? Paid *la cuenta*? He couldn't remember. Some detective.

"And I want to thank you, Mr. Skopakos, for contacting the car rental people to pick up my car." Mrs. Arnold smiled. "I'm very impressed that they will be dropping off another car for me here at the hotel tomorrow."

"I would have been delighted to provide transportation back to Cancun for you," he replied, "but alas, we will be heading on to Merida tomorrow morning and then on to Progreso. My yacht is anchored there waiting to take me on the next leg of my voyage."

"And where would that be?" Sam tried to make the question casual, though the fact that he hadn't spoken to the Greek throughout the meal made it difficult.

Skapakos seemed unfazed as he replied. "We'll be going to Tampa, Florida."

It was all Sam could do not to say "Aha!"

**M**aggie loved the old Spanish hacienda style of the hotel with its wide verandahs overlooking the pool. She'd have wished they were on the second floor except they'd never have managed to get Jennifer up the stairs. But she'd seen the lush blooms of the Jacaranda trees at the end of the pillared corridors and heard the palm trees whispering overhead. It was perfect.

If she hadn't still been worried about Jennifer, Maggie would really have revelled in this room – especially their bathroom. It was huge, and a quarter of it was a jacuzzi. There was even a bidet, but the best part was the amazing stained glass window featuring a toucan and an egret on one side and a profusion of jungle flowers on the other. She supposed she should enjoy it while she could before Jen recovered enough to mess it up.

She was sitting on Jennifer's bed. There was a blood-stained towel on the pillow now. She'd done her best to rinse the blood out of Jennifer's hair. Hard to do when you can't see the head – or the hair.

"So," Jennifer was saying, her voice was weak but at least she was sounding more like herself now, "I guess I'm stuck being invisible all the time we're here..."

Maggie nodded. "Everybody thinks you're back at Chichen Itza."

"So when I can get out of here...walk around okay, I mean," Jennifer continued, "first thing I do will be to get close to Brady and hope I catch him talking to the Greek Tycoon. I'm dying to know what that man is doing here."

"Oh, he probably just happens to be in the vicinity. Just cruisin' around the world. Doing his Greek Tycoon thing." I am not going to get Jennifer all excited speculating on some spy scenario, Maggie thought.

Jennifer's voice was indignant. "Sure, Maggie! So what's the connection to Brady? I suppose you expect me to believe that Brady and Conchita whatsit were hitchhiking and the kindly Tycoon gave them a lift in his limo?"

"Jennifer!" Maggie had decided to busy herself hanging up the outfit she was going to wear tomorrow. "Next thing you'll be telling me, this Elefterious Skopakos is some sort of Greek James Bond!"

"Wow! Maggie!" Jennifer sounded impressed. "You could be onto something! It would explain the ladies' man reputation. The yacht, the constant international travel — obviously he'd have to have a girl in every port. It's his cover!"

Maggie stared at the bed in horror. Sometimes her twin was just too much. "I hope you're laughing Jennifer...you can't be serious. Ooops! Don't laugh. I didn't mean that. You've got to stay invisible.

"I'm in no mood for laughing now anyway. My head still hurts." Jennifer sounded rueful. "I wonder how long I can stay invisible. We've never tested the spell you know…to see how long it would last, I mean."

Maggie had been thinking the same thing. She sighed. "We'll just have to hope it will stay."

"Look on the bright side," Jennifer said. "At least Grand won't have to pay an admission fee for me at the site tomorrow!"

Obviously she's recovered, Maggie thought. She hadn't known how worried she was until the relief flooded over her. "It's good to see that you're getting back to normal," she said; "Sam will be so relieved."

"Sam?" Jennifer's usual smartass tone was there. "Sam wouldn't care. Don't you know Sam cares about 'the Lovely Maggie'? Really Muggins, it's plain as day. The guy thinks you're terrific."

Maggie just stared at the pillow. "Don't be silly, Jennifer, he's had a crush on you since you two were in kindergarten. Why do you think he goes along with all your crazy schemes? Not to mention the screwball Arnold & Elwin Detective Agency."

Maggie was beginning to be annoyed. It was so obvious. Why couldn't Jennifer see it? Sam was really a smart, sensible guy. The only explanation for his going along with Jennifer's nutty ideas was because he cared about her.

"Hmmm," said Jennifer. "Obviously we should have had this talk a long time ago. I've been staying out of it, thinking I'd be in the way. Why do you think I agreed for you to be the bathing beauty assistant in the magic act?"

"Because I couldn't very well be the invisible assistant who made everything happen!" Maggie said curtly.

"Hah!" said Jennifer. "Right! I did all the work and Sam just stood there ogling you, his pinky slinky 'Lovely' assistant!"

"I do believe you're jealous!" Maggie was laughing now. Unfortunately, so was Jennifer.

Maggie watched as Jennifer's hands and feet appeared. First to go, first to come back. Soon there were legs, arms, and a body lying on the bed. Jennifer's tousled hair appeared on the pillow.

The upside, Maggie thought, would be that Grand could examine that head wound. She would definitely be relieved to be able to do that. Everything was back now except for Jennifer's face. Always the last to come.

"I guess," Jennifer said, lips appearing as she spoke, "that I can always tell a lie in the morning before we leave for the site."

There was a knock at the door. "Who is it?" Maggie called, giving Jennifer the "Sssh" sign.

She heard her grandmother's voice and opened the door a crack until she was sure it was just her and Sam.

"Being cautious, are you? That's good," said Sam as they entered. "Oh, oh!" he spotted Jennifer on the bed. "She's back! Weren't you going to stay out of sight?"

"She laughed." Maggie said. "It was an accident."

"We were talking about you," Jennifer grinned. "Very amusing!"

Their grandmother looked relieved. "Let me see that head of yours, my girl."

Jennifer obediently sat up while her grandmother parted the tangled hair.

"It's really not too bad," she said. "I wish I had some hydrogen peroxide though."

"Oh yes," laughed Maggie. "Jennifer could have a nice blond streak!"

Jennifer ignored her. "I'll be fine, Grand. After I've eaten I'll go take a shower and wash the blood out of my hair properly." She reached for the tray her grandmother had brought in. "So tell us what happened at dinner. Any more clues?"

Maggie picked up a tortilla and spread some filling on it. She'd leave most of the food for Jennifer. She wasn't that hungry. Sam was explaining that the Greek Tycoon would be leaving tomorrow.

"It's just as well, I think," said Grand. "I think he's a bit suspicious of me. He told me he was very impressed by the way I not only disarmed our friend with the woolen hat but knocked him out at the same time. Said I must have moved very quickly as he hadn't seen it happen at all!"

Sam looked up, surprised. "I didn't hear that!"

Maggie could see that amused her grandmother.

"Oh, I suspect that was when you were deep in conversation with your friend Chita!" she said.

Maggie and Jennifer spoke as one. "Chita?"

Maggie had never seen Sam move so quickly. He turned and fled for the door.

"You can run but you can't hide," Jennifer called wickedly as the door closed behind him.

Jennifer was feeling much better by morning. And she was invisible again. It hadn't been difficult.

"I'm so sorry," Grand had said as she and Maggie were leaving to knock on Sam's door and go for a late breakfast, "that you won't be able to eat. But," she promised, "we'll get the hotel kitchen to pack a sandwich lunch so we can picnic at the site."

"Not a problem," Jennifer had said. "I'm not a bit hungry."

That had been a huge lie. She'd been, and still was, ravenous. No lunch yesterday and that little daub of supper she'd had to share with Maggie. The lack of food hadn't bothered her then, she was still feeling woozy, but now she was fine – and starving. And invisible once more.

She risked opening the door and slipping out into the hall. Not exactly a hall – really a long balcony. Rooms on one side, overlooking the pool and terrace restaurant on the other. There was nobody seated at the far tables – those that could be seen from their doorway. No one could have seen the door open. Even if they had, they would only think someone had opened it and then changed his or her mind about coming out. And there was nobody in the corridor. She went silently down the stairs and followed the little stepping stones to the terrace. Several people were sitting at the tables on the shady side. Grand and Sam and Maggie would still be getting their food inside. But tucked between two pillars sat Brady and the Señorita. Sam's Chita was looking splendid, this time wearing a low-cut red dress. Not really breakfast wear, but it definitely emphasized the glittering necklace she wore.

Jennifer decided to move over and listen. She'd just got into position when she realized there were people seated at the table beyond. It was tucked into a little space between two hibiscus bushes. Hadn't Sam said that the two Greeks were leaving first thing this morning? It was well past ten and there they were. Were they watching Brady? Or was Brady watching them?

Anyway, from where she stood, she could watch them all. She wasn't sure if she could hear them, though. Right now they were just sitting, eating. Or at least the men were. The Señorita was fiddling with her coffee spoon. Tapping it against her coffee cup. Was it some kind of code? Click, click, click.... click. She obviously couldn't make dots and dashes. The pause between taps must mean something.

Why didn't Brady stop her?

The Greek Tycoon was waving at the waiter now. "Bring the car," he commanded, and Alekos left the table. "*La cuenta, por favor,*" he said as the waiter neared. He signed and left.

Strange, thought Jennifer, he's being very careful not to go by Brady's table. You'd think he would say good-bye at least.

She didn't have much time to think about it. The Señorita was getting up too.

"I need to visit the Ladies'," she spoke curtly to Brady.

He looked at her suspiciously. Then he got up from the table and followed her, leaning against the wall across from the door. Jennifer managed to slip inside before the door closed behind the Señorita.

Maybe she really just does have to use the room. I shouldn't be so suspicious, Jennifer thought. But when Conchita de Lapiz came out she held a folded sheet of paper in her hand. She checked the other cubicles and then tucked it behind the paper towel dispenser, washed her hands and left.

Now what to do? Obviously this was a drop and somebody would be along to pick up the note.

Should I take the note or just read it and leave it there? I can't take it very far, somebody would notice a piece of paper floating around.

She'd have to get Maggie, she decided.

She wiggled the paper out. She'd read it first. Luckily there wasn't much written there. 10:30 and a few Spanish words. Just three words, but she didn't know them. Maybe Maggie would.

The door was opening, somebody would be coming in. Jennifer slipped the paper in leaving a tiny corner out to remove it later. A blonde lady with a little girl in tow was coming in. They were slow enough that Jennifer was able to slip out before the door closed behind them. Now to find Maggie and see if she could read that note.

Maggie had just settled down to a breakfast of tamales and bread when Jennifer jabbed her in the back.

Really, Muggins, you shouldn't jump like that, Jennifer thought, people will suspect something. She poked again. This time Maggie was ready for it. She turned and glared but just kept eating. Drastic times call for drastic measures, Jennifer decided. She grabbed Maggie's arm causing her to drop her fork. As she reached under the table Jennifer hissed in her ear, "Come with me. Now!"

Maggie must have realized Jennifer wouldn't let up. "Excuse me," she said to Sam and Grand.

She couldn't exactly follow Jennifer, but Jen's hand was firmly in her back pushing her along, out of the restaurant toward the restroom. But there was a sign on the door now. *Cerrado*/Closed. And a janitor's cart parked outside.

"Try the door, Maggie," Jennifer whispered. "Something fishy here."

Maggie pushed the door open, a man's voice, "No! Señorita. *Prohibido el paso...*" and in a heavy accent. "You can not come in!" Maggie stayed where she was in the doorway but Jennifer slipped by her and went around to where the sink was. A man in a janitor's coverall was busily prying the paper towel holder away from the wall, cursing softly.

Jennifer moved soundlessly back to Maggie, whispered "Wait!" and went back in as the door closed. She had to see what became of the paper. It had fallen down and lay on the floor beside the garbage container. Would the man find it?

He certainly had no interest in cleaning the bathroom, even though that was his ploy. By now he had the towel dispenser pulled away from the wall and was ripping all the towels out, tossing them around. Very inconsiderate, thought Jennifer. Somebody's going to have to clean up this mess. She watched, not daring to breathe in case he could

hear her. Once, he did look around as if he had sensed someone behind him, but having finished his attack on the dispenser he glanced down, spotted the note, picked it up and
left.

But not before Jennifer had a close look. It was definitely
not Woolen Hat without his cap. This man was taller and
thinner. Same swarthy skin and moustache like hundreds of
others. But when he went by her as he left she could see his
face was pock-marked or at least that the pores were very
enlarged. Craters, she thought. I'll recognize him if I see
him again but I'll have to get very close.

Maggie opened the door, took a look at the mess, and
hissed, "Jennifer! What's this all about?"

"Never mind," she said. "Let's get out of here before
somebody comes in and blames *you*."

Jennifer was surprised to see that Brady and the Señorita
had stopped on their way out of the restaurant and were
talking to Grand and Sam. Maybe not so strange. After all
they'd arrived together and had dinner last night. All the
more reason for them to appear acquainted. And, she
thought, all the more reason that it was strange the way
Skopakos and Stavros' brother had left without a word to
anyone.

She wondered if they had actually left at all.

**F**inally, thought Sam, we're going to see Uxmal. Brunch had been delicious, but then they'd had to wait for Maggie to finish eating because she'd been interrupted. And they'd had a little chat with Brady and Chita, who was looking lovelier than ever with that million dollar smile – and necklace. Once they'd left, she told them about Jennifer being invisible again.

Sam was carrying the lunch in his back pack, his camera around his neck. As soon as they left the hotel and were out of earshot of anyone, Jennifer started bugging him.

"I saw you buy a chocolate bar in the gift shop..." her voice hissed in his ear. "It was for me, right? Please, please, please...I'm starving."

Reluctantly Sam pulled the bar out and began unwrapping it as they walked over to the site. He hoped nobody would wonder why he was still hungry when he'd just eaten. He barely escaped having his fingers bitten as half of the bar was chomped away.

"Too much for you to wait for lunch, I suppose?" He teased.

"I'm starving...starve...starve...starve." Definite chocolate breath in his face as she spoke. "So unwrap the rest of
that bar pronto, pardner."

Sam smiled and watched the bar disappear out of his
hand. Good thing nobody was nearby all right.

There was lots to see even before you went in. The best
selection of souvenirs and т-shirts he'd seen since he got to
Mexico. He could see Maggie was itching to look at the
embroidered dresses, but they decided to wait until after
they'd toured the site. Once inside, there was a courtyard
with shops and a museum. He and Maggie were fascinated
by the scale models of all the major sites in the Yucatan.
Fun to look at the tiny version of the things they'd seen at
Coba. He looked for the site he'd be going to tomorrow
when Grandad came to pick him up, but Sayil wasn't there.
Too small, or not enough excavated yet, he supposed.
There were, he knew, dozens of Mayan sites on the
Yucatan peninsula, many still hidden in the jungle. He'd
counted nearly forty in the Tourist Guidebook map
Jennifer had been looking at when they set out from
Chichen Itza.

They walked up the steps onto the site. The huge pyramid in front of them was called the Pyramid of the
Magician.

"Listen to this!" Maggie had her face in the Uxmal
guidebook. "The pyramid was built over a period of three
hundred years." She pointed. "Five different temples set on
top of one another. Though it says here that temples I and
II were completely hidden by Temple III, which then
became just a base for Temple IV. You can sort of see it rising out of the lower one, can't you!"

"Yes," Grand nodded. "It reminds me a bit of the Step Pyramid of Djoser at Sakkara near Cairo."

Someday I'll have done so much travelling that I'll be able to say stuff like that, thought Sam. "So why's it called the Temple of the Magician?" He asked as they walked along the pathway toward it.

"Apparently," laughed Maggie, "a witch succeeded in hatching a child from an egg. It grew up to be a dwarf whom the witch sent to challenge the King of Uxmal. The King set several tasks which the dwarf accomplished with the help of his mother's magic. One of them was to build an enormous palace in one night or face execution." She waved her arms at it as Sam snapped her picture.

"Right!" said Jennifer. "A three-hundred-year night!" Her voice changed to wonderment. "Look! Iguanas!"

It was true. There beside the pathway the grass was dotted with burrows, and sunning themselves were four or five huge iguanas. He went closer to get a picture and they quickly disappeared down the holes.

"This is perfect!" Jennifer's voice was enthusiastic. "Okay if I just stay here, Grand? I'll bet they'll come out again if they can't see anyone. Besides," she lowered her voice conspiratorially, "I can keep watch and see if anybody we know shows up and warn you."

Good thing we're together, Sam thought, and nobody's close enough to notice that one of the voices isn't coming from one of us.

"Here," said Maggie, holding out the guidebook with its plan of the site. She ran her finger along the way. "We'll be here exploring this, then we'll go over here to the courtyard called The Nun's Quadrangle...apparently the Spaniards thought all the little rooms were like a convent...and then we'll cut through the Ballgame Court and up to the House of the Turtles and the Governor's Palace." She paused. "Then, I guess we could come back and get you...if you haven't come after us."

"Remember lunch?" said Jennifer. "I'm famished! That tour you've got planned sounds like it might take a long time, Maggie. I could have died of starvation by then."

"We'll just do the Nun's Quadrangle," her grandmother said, "there's plenty there to see. Then we'll come back. We can have lunch by the House of the Governor. I'm sure we can find a private spot so we don't have to worry about sandwiches being devoured in mid-air!"

Sam and Maggie checked out the Puuc carvings on the Pyramid. "I guess those are the carvings, the guide book refers to...of the rain god Chac." He was getting lots of pictures. He hoped he'd recognize what they were later on.

The place was filling with tourists now. A group, evidently from Germany, were following their German-speaking tour guide. Sam took pictures of Grand and Maggie beside some of the carvings. He tried to get a shot of the whole building, hard to do without slanting the camera and shooting up.

"What did Brady say when you told him about the note?" Maggie asked Grand as they walked along the top of the Nun's Quadrangle.

The group of tourists had followed along the other side. No one to hear them, unless someone was hiding in one of the many little "cells" built along the sides. Sam checked into the two closest in the row near them. The first was empty, the second was too, if you didn't count a pile of rubble and a canvas covering some chicken wire and other material probably used to patch the crumbling stone. They were alone. He moved back to hear Mrs. Arnold's reply.

"He was most interested." She smiled at Maggie. "He was glad to know you'd left it in place. Conchita's contact won't know it was intercepted."

"So he thinks that the contact is at the Sound and Light Show?" Maggie asked. "It starts at 9."

Sam remembered that there was a special show this evening. They already had their tickets. He wasn't sure if it was a dramatization or just a narrative of the history of the Mayans at Uxmal.

"Thanks to you and Jennifer he can be prepared for the meeting. I don't think he's working alone but it's just as well that we don't know who else is involved." She looked sternly at the two of them. "We are not going to get mixed up in this! We've already been seen with him...we don't want his opponents to think we're part of what he's doing here."

People were streaming up onto the walkway behind them. Sam raised his camera and snapped a few pictures. He wanted to get the row of little rooms with their arched entrances. He wished he'd taken the shot earlier when he could have avoided some of the tour group who were coming in. He might try again later, though at the rate it was filling up he figured he wouldn't stand much chance of finding the place empty.

"We'd better get a move on," said Maggie, leading the way down the steps to the grassy area in the centre of the quadrangle. "I'm surprised Jennifer hasn't showed up looking for us...or for the lunch."

"She'd never make it up the stairs through that crowd," Sam laughed, "but I bet she'll be waiting."

They walked through the archway. The neat little map in Maggie's guidebook was deceptive, Sam decided. It was quite a walk to the ball court. And he was beginning to think that when you'd seen one ball court you'd seen them all.

They were heading back to get Jennifer when somebody bumped into Sam. Since there was no one there he said, "Hi, Jennifer."

"Very busy today," she panted. "I'll bet a couple of hundred people came in.

"Anyone interesting?" asked Maggie.

"No woolen hats...but I think maybe the fake janitor came in. He was dressed differently, of course, and I couldn't really get close enough to be sure."

Jennifer picked the lunch spot. It was a lovely private place under the trees across from the House of the Governor. It was far enough from the path that they could talk but they could see anyone coming. The tourists were getting tired by the time they came by on the way to the far pyramids.

Maggie was impressed with the choice. "The Governor's Palace," she read, "was universally acclaimed as one of the finest examples of Mayan architecture. And," she added, "this expert named Bernal ranks it among the most beautiful monuments on the American Continent."

Jennifer hadn't explained that she'd chosen the spot because she wanted to look at the statue of the jaguar in the square in front. It was roped off so that you couldn't get close enough to touch it. But she would.

She sat behind Maggie so that nobody would notice the sandwiches disappearing in mid-air, bite by bite. There was nobody close anyway. The ham and cheese sandwiches were quite ordinary – good enough — but the tomato ones were delicious. They were a bit soggy and squashed from being in

Sam's backpack, but Jennifer liked them soggy, which was good because nobody else did and she got to eat them all. Which meant that she was the last to finish and she was feeling a bit stuffed. The last thing she wanted to do was wander around looking at pyramids and listening to Sam and Maggie rave about Puuc carvings and all their 'Ec people. What she wanted now was a nice little nap right here in this shady spot.

To her surprise, Grand agreed.

"I'm going to sit on that bench across the square and relax while Maggie and Sam explore. Everyone can meet there in an hour." She laughed, "I won't exactly be able to watch you, Jennifer, but I can watch this place in case somebody comes by and steps on you!"

The others left and Jennifer curled up and studied the jaguar statue. She smiled. She had plans for it later, but right now she'd just get a bit of shut-eye.

She was wakened by voices. Close by. There was a boot right beside her head. She rolled over and tried to wiggle away. Two of the security guards who patrolled the place were standing under the trees smoking. One of them flicked his cigarette butt over. It landed on her leg and she swatted it away.

Ouch! That smarted. Lucky for me, Jennifer thought, that didn't happen while I was lying there asleep. I'd have yelled for sure.

Of course, she couldn't understand what the two men were saying. They were speaking Spanish. But she didn't like the way they were looking over to the bench where Grand sat. She wondered why Grand hadn't come over when the men arrived. Hadn't that been the plan? But Maggie and

Sam were there and Maggie was showing Grand something in that stupid Guidebook of hers so maybe Grand hadn't noticed.

Then she recognized one word. "De Lapiz."

So they were talking about the Señorita. And they were definitely looking at Grand. Was there a connection as far as these people were concerned? They must think there was a connection between the Señorita and Grand. Maybe they'd seen them arriving at the hotel, or in the restaurant last night.

Jennifer decided it was time for a distraction. Silently she slipped away across the grass toward the jaguar statue. The ropes around it were easy to jump. She wished Sam could get a picture of her now – sitting on an ancient jaguar's back. Now to do something to draw the guards attention away from Grand.

Luckily she'd tied her hair back with a red bandana this morning. Quickly she untied it and waved it in the air. Stupid! As long as she held on it wouldn't show. She tied it around the jaguar's neck and let go.

The guards didn't notice a thing, but a man and woman were walking by with a couple of children in tow. The littlest one, Jennifer guessed at two or three years old, spotted it right away.

"Look at the doggie!"

Jennifer almost laughed. It was true. The statue did look like somebody's pet with a trendy collar. Everybody was pointing and the guards were finally paying attention.

She wasn't about to laugh now. They were running this way and she'd better clear out. Get over to Grand and the others and get them away before the guards had finished. She gave the jaguar one last pat.

"Good boy!" she whispered and fled.

She was over to the bench when Maggie noticed the jaguar. "Jennifer!" She groaned.

"Oh dear!" said Grand.

Sam didn't say a word. His camera was up, getting a shot of the jaguar just as the two guards rushed up, glaring at the people who were closest to it.

Once again Jennifer had to squelch a laugh. Not hard to do. Her voice was deadly serious as she grabbed Maggie by the arm. "Come on, Grand! Everybody clear out while they're undressing the jaguar. Those guys may be guards but they're on to something. They were talking about Señorita de Lapiz, *and* they were looking at you!"

To her relief there was no arguing. Grand was up off the bench leading them down the path away from the bench to the place that was marked Quadrangle of the Doves on Maggie's plan. From there they doubled back behind the House of the Turtles. Jennifer looked up at the little turtle figures sculpted along the frieze. At least the Spaniards named that one right, she thought.

"We will," said Grand, panting a little, "cut back through the Ball Court to the Entrance. I think it's time we went back to the hotel. Perhaps a rest would do us all good before dinner."

Jennifer kept looking back. Those guards would have had a much shorter distance to cover to the entrance once they'd removed the jaguar's scarf but there was no sign of them. Perhaps they'd continued their patrol. Or were still looking around the pyramids for Grand and Sam and Maggie. She was glad she was invisible. She couldn't wait to see what would happen when Brady and the Señorita arrived tonight. Were the guards part of Brady's back-up, she wondered? Or were they part of the Señorita's gang come to pick up the diamonds? Either way she couldn't figure out why they'd been so interested in Grand. Could it be they were really looking at Sam? Was his camera still attracting attention? She'd forgotten all about Señor Woolen Hat.

**W**hen they arrived back that evening for the show, they were led across in front of the Pyramid of the Magician, around the back, and up the narrow winding steps to the Nuns Quadrangle. Maggie could see that rows of chairs had been placed along the length of the nearest side facing into the open area of the quadrangle. Electric spotlights beamed all along the route they had come and showed the wall opposite them. Beyond that the site was pitch black.

The dark came so quickly in the Yucatan. So different from home in Northern Alberta. No twilight here. No shadows or outlines – just sudden pitch darkness. Everything was swallowed up by it.

Sam was leading the way. He found them four seats just in from the beginning of the second row. Maggie sat next to him. They'd wondered what to do about Jennifer. There was always a danger of somebody noticing an empty seat and coming and sitting on her. Grand had thrown her shawl over the chair between herself and Maggie. Then if anybody asked they'd say it was occupied. Absolutely true. Grand was sitting on the end of the row. A good spot – they could watch for Brady and the Señorita to arrive.

"But," Grand had warned yet again, "we will merely watch to see what happens. We are here to see the show, not to interfere with Mr. Brady's plans, whatever they are!"

Maggie knew the warning was for Jennifer. She also knew that Grand might as well whistle in the wind. But at least with Jennifer sitting between herself and Grand she wouldn't be able to sneak out. Climbing over the back of the chair was out of the question, she'd be bumping the people behind. Maggie smiled. Invisible or not, Jennifer was trapped.

She adjusted her headset. They'd each been given earphones and a headset. Clever. That way people could listen to the narration in whatever language they wished. Grand was holding her headset onto just one ear. Maggie realized she was letting Jennifer listen to the other side. Not that Jennifer would care all that much.

Now the lights were being dimmed. Again she was amazed at how dark it was. It would be hard to get up and move out once everyone was seated. A couple of late-comers were squeezing into the front row. Maggie squinted, trying to see. A man and a woman. The dim lights were reflected in her necklace.

She felt Jennifer lean close to her. "Brady and the Señorita," she hissed. Maggie nodded and nudged Sam.

The show began.

It wasn't a live performance, of course. Lights played on the walls opposite or lit up the buildings beyond and the narration began telling of the great city of Uxmal and how the Mayans had built it. There were three great cities:

Uxmal, Mayapan and Chichen Itza. Maggie especially liked the lovely romantic story about how the Prince of Chichen had fallen for the daughter of the King of Uxmal and been refused her hand. But the Princess had fled with her lover. She hoped they'd lived happily ever after, though the narrator didn't bother to say that. There'd been wars between rival cities, but mostly the enemy of the Maya had been drought. The music swelled as voices cried out.

"Chaac...chaac...chaac..."

The people were beseeching the Rain God to help them. But the drought continued and the wells dried up and the people were forced to leave.

As the narration ended, she reached over to grab Jennifer. There was nobody there. And Grand was gone too. Strange. They must have gone looking for a restroom. Or decided to get ahead of the crowd.

"Sam?" Thank goodness he was still there beside her. "Did Grand say anything about meeting us at the entrance?"

He shook his head. The lights were coming up now. Ahead of them Brady and the Señorita were getting up to leave. The diamonds still sparkled around her neck. So, Maggie thought, nothing had happened. Yet.

Frankly she didn't care now. The lights had come back on, lighting everything, as the crowd began to make its way to the exit.

She forgot to watch to see if anyone came to grab the Señorita's necklace, but when the lights came up she could see no sign of Grand. Wherever she is, Jennifer had better be with her, Maggie thought. Then she had to concentrate getting down the narrow stairs. People were crammed up in a bottleneck at the second landing. Jennifer would have to be out of the way or she'd be crushed.

She kept checking to be sure Sam was close. Once, for a minute or two, they got separated and she couldn't see him. When they got close again, she gave up and grabbed his hand. She wasn't about to lose him too.

Once out beside the Magician's Pyramid people began to fan out.

"Let's climb up the steps a bit and see if we can see Grand." It was where they'd climbed before to see the carving of Chaac.

They hadn't gone far when she felt Jennifer grab her arm. Jennifer! Thank goodness.

"Where's Grand?"

"Gone!" Jennifer's voice sounded frantic. "She was sitting beside me and then suddenly I felt her getting up to talk to someone...she left the headset but when I looked she was gone!" Tears in her voice now. "I looked around but it was so dark while the show was on. I thought I'd come here and watch. She'd have to come along the stairways past here when it was over...but she didn't...she hasn't...not yet!"

Maggie's chest clenched tight like a fist. She knew she could let go of Sam's hand now but there was no way she was going to.

People were still spilling out of the stairways down onto the pathways and the lawns beyond. Maggie strained her eyes looking, but there was no sign of Grand.

"She wouldn't have gone without us," Jennifer's voice was calmer now.

"Of course not!" Maggie was absolutely sure of that. "We have to turn in these headsets." Maggie waved hers and the other headset that dangled from her arm along with Grand's shawl she'd picked up on the way out. "Remember? They made her hand over her driver's license as security." They'd driven over from the hotel, not wanting to walk in the dark.

"Would she have gone to the entrance?" Sam suggested. "Maybe waiting for us there?"

"Doubtful," said Maggie.

"Couldn't have...I've been here watching all the time," from Jennifer. "Tell you what though, you wait here, keep watching, and I'll go to the entrance and see if she's there. If she is she'll be waiting by the headset counter.

They could hear her starting down the stairs. She'd better be quieter than that if she doesn't want to be noticed, thought Maggie.

Sam had adjusted his camera and was snapping pictures of the people as they flowed by. The crowd was beginning to dwindle now.

"Come on, Sam, we'd better move before Security comes by and kicks us out. Maybe we can duck into one of the alcoves down below and still keep watch." Maggie started down the steps.

"You're right," he followed her. "Soon they'll notice if people are wandering around." They were at the bottom now, beginning to edge around the side of the building.

Backing up while pretending to be part of a bunch of people going forward was not as easy as the movies make it look, Maggie decided. Twice she stumbled and might have fallen if Sam hadn't grabbed her arm. At last they were hidden.

"Oh, oh," said Maggie, "how's Jennifer going to find us here?"

"She couldn't," came Jennifer's voice from around the corner, "unless she happened to see you doing your comedy back-up routine."

Good for Jennifer, Maggie thought. "Any sign of Grand?"

"No...let me get my breath," Jennifer panted. "That's quite a run. She wasn't there. You're lucky you didn't go back, I had to crawl under the turnstile to get back in and nearly got trampled."

"Now what do we do?" asked Maggie. "No point in reporting her missing...not if the guards are in on some sort of conspiracy. We don't know who the Good Guys are!"

"And," added Jennifer, "they'd probably have you and Sam sitting around in a room somewhere. I want you out here with me!"

"I guess," said Sam, "we just wait until everyone's left and the place is shut down and then we search."

"She's got to be here." Maggie couldn't keep the despair out of her voice.

**O**f course it was Jennifer who fell over the body. Sam might have known.

Jennifer had argued that they shouldn't expand the search beyond the Nun's quadrangle. She was positive that her grandmother couldn't have left that area without being seen. But he and Maggie had convinced her to go out through the archway to the Ball Court and search behind the walls. After all, there was another exit.

She was rushing ahead of Sam and Maggie in the darkness. They heard a thud and an "Ooof".

"Watch where you're going Jennifer!" Maggie hissed. "Someone will hear us."

"Shut-up Maggie! There's nobody out here...except..." Her voice was louder. "Stop, you guys! Sam, turn on that flashlight...there's somebody...."

Sam was quick with the flashlight – they couldn't see Jennifer, of course. But one of her white sandals had come off and was lying on top of the body of a man. He was face down on the stones.

"Is he...?"

Maggie was on her way to turn him over when Sam stopped her. There was the hilt of a knife showing in the man's back buried in a plaid shirt. Sam flicked the flashlight to his head. It was turned so that they could see one cheek. The skin was distinctive, marked by enlarged pores. Next to him a black evening bag lay open. It was empty.

"I don't think we should touch him..." Sam whispered, "...and I think we should get out of here fast."

They heard Jennifer scramble to her feet. The sandal was snatched off and floated away. "Turn off the light quick, Sam," she whispered, "whoever did it might still be here!

"The grounds have been closed since five o'clock and nobody would come here while the show was on...he could have been here for a long time...ever since this afternoon anyway," he protested.

Sam was trying to be calm – someone needed to be calm and it wasn't likely to be Jennifer. But Jennifer had grabbed him by the arm and was pushing him and Maggie away, back along the path, hard to see now that he'd switched off the flashlight.

"He could have been..." her voice seemed to catch in her throat "...but...but...he's still warm!"

They could just see enough in the dim light to head back into the nun's courtyard.

After everyone left they'd waited – it seemed forever – for the floodlights to be turned off and the two guards to do a final check. Luckily, a few dim lights were left on. And luckily, Sam had tucked Maggie's flashlight in his backpack. They used it sparingly, in case it attracted attention.

"Shouldn't we tell somebody... about the dead man?" Maggie panted as she ran after them.

No answer from Jennifer. They entered the courtyard through one of the side doors and leaned against the wall. Jennifer's breath was coming in sob-like gasps.

"It's okay...okay...Jen..." Maggie comforted. "You're okay now."

Not really, thought Sam. We've lost your grandmother... somebody's been murdered, and we're locked in here for the night with the killer...the killers, perhaps. Hardly okay.

## JENNIFER (30)

**J**ennifer's bare foot was killing her. Not being able to see the crushed stones or pebbles on the pathways was terrible. She hobbled along still carrying the sandal. Stupid. She might as well wear it. Either way it showed. But it didn't matter right now. Later on if she needed to sneak up on someone she could take it off.

Somewhere here in the dark there was a killer. And Grand.

"It's too bad," said Sam, "that we can't keep an eye on the body, in case the killer comes back."

"Bad idea," said Maggie. "Even Jennifer couldn't see anything. It's so dark over there."

"Well..." Jennifer said. "They'd probably have flashlights...."

Sam shone the flashlight on his watch. "It's nearly two o'clock. I don't think the guards are bothering to patrol inside any more. They're probably just sitting around the entrance. We've got to keep searching."

"Should we check all those little rooms along the sides again?" Maggie couldn't hide the discouragement in her voice. "Maybe we missed one."

Jennifer's teeth were chattering, it was amazing how it cooled off at night. Sam had brought a jacket and Maggie had a sweater, but Jennifer couldn't put one on when they left for the evening. It would have showed.

"Here," Maggie said holding Grand's shawl out in the general direction of the chattering teeth. "Now you'll be a shawl and one shoe drifting about in the night."

"Th...thanks." Jennifer wrapped the shawl around her. Much better. "I think there are some little rooms down here." She said trying to sound positive. "We could try there." Nobody had dared mention why, if Mrs. Arnold was in one of the rooms, she didn't call out. Nobody wanted to talk about it. The best possible scenario was that Grand was tied up as a hostage or something. The worst – well she couldn't even think about that.

And she hadn't even told Maggie and Sam about the diamonds – yet.

She wasn't sure she'd done the right thing grabbing the necklace. Had she messed up the way she almost did with the note in the Ladies Room?

It was while she was watching for Grand to leave the show. Brady and the Señorita had come along. Conchita de Lapiz didn't show up so well now in her black dress. Nothing sparkled about her neck. Had she made the drop?

But as Jennifer watched, the Señorita moved toward the steps of the Magician's pyramid not far from Jennifer, dropped her little black evening bag, kicked it behind a crumbling piece of stone from the steps, and then stepped back holding onto Brady as she pretended to shake a pebble out of her high-heeled sandal.

Jennifer had been able to slip down, snap the little beaded purse open and slip the diamond necklace further away, scooping dirt and pebbles over it. Just in time too, for she had just closed the clasp again when the purse was snatched away from her hand. It happened so quickly she saw nothing but the back of man in a plaid shirt as he ducked back into the crowd.

She remembered her triumphant feeling fading as she waited for Grand. First she couldn't wait to tell her. Then as she thought about it, she began to worry. What had she done? Obviously Brady meant the drop to be made. Would his and the Señorita's life be endangered when the jewels weren't there? Grand had told her not to get involved. She'd dreaded having to tell. And then there had been no Grand to tell. She'd almost forgotten the stupid necklace. She supposed she'd better tell Maggie and Sam now.

"At least," Maggie said, as the flashlight probed the darkness in one of the little rooms, "your grandfather is coming tomorrow, Sam...we'll have somebody we can trust to talk to...somebody to help us...."

She was interrupted by voices outside. Another patrol? Sam switched off the flashlight. Judging by the voices they were above, and anyone up there might not have noticed yet.

Jennifer slipped off the shawl and sandal and thrust them into his hands. Hardly daring to breathe, she found her way to the steps to go up and see what was going on.

Sam and Maggie could do nothing but stay hidden.

To Jennifer's amazement the two men on the walkway above her were speaking English. They were dressed in guard's uniforms, but she doubted they were the same men as this afternoon. More of the same gang? Or some of Brady's men? She swallowed a whimper of pain when she stubbed her toe on the steps as she tried to get closer.

"He says that the handover was made as they were leaving," said the one lighting a cigarette.

For a moment the match flared, illuminating a hat she knew. Jennifer gasped.

Instantly two flashlight beams crisscrossed the stairway she stood on.

"You hear that?" The other man demanded.

"Probably we've disturbed some of the birds...this place is full of swallows." Señor Woolen Hat blew a smoke ring.

"And the drop was a fake? Jose didn't stash the stuff somewhere before we got to him?"

"No time." The other man's voice seemed full of fury. "We risked Montero's rage by killing his man to get those damned diamonds and had no luck. Still," he seemed to calm down a bit, "we *can* bargain. We've got that woman who was talking to that phoney DEA agent. She claimed she didn't know anything and maybe she didn't, but she'll do for a deal to get the diamonds. He might claim he's already paid for the merchandise but we didn't get any payment and he'd better come through or the lady's...."

Jennifer shuddered as the man made a slashing motion across his throat. She didn't dare breathe.

She'd really done it this time. Because of her, Grand was kidnapped. She watched as the men turned and walked back past the rows of chairs they and the audience had sat in earlier. As silently as she could she limped after them. Maybe they'd lead her to Grand. But at the foot of the stairs they separated. One walked toward the brightly lit exit and the other, the one she'd recognized as Señor Woolen Hat, went over and leaned against a tree by the iguana's patch of lawn. From where he stood he had a very good view of the area around the Magician's pyramid where the drop had been made and where, thanks to her, the diamonds still lay. Jennifer turned back to report what she'd heard – and confess to Sam and Maggie what she'd done.

am stared open-mouthed in the direction of Jennifer's voice as she confessed her part in the diamond switch. She was sobbing when she finished. He waited for Maggie to say something critical. Jennifer really had messed up this time. Or had she?

He decided it would be best to butt in before Maggie got going.

"But your grandmother was already gone long before the drop, wasn't she?" Sam put in. "We saw Brady and the Señorita going out with the crowd. You said you were watching to see if she showed up."

He could see Maggie nodding as she moved to the doorway of their little cell, holding out the shawl to Jennifer. "That's right, Jen," she said, "Obviously one of those guards you just heard...came and lured Grand away...remember? You said you heard someone speaking to her before you thought she left to go to the *sanitario*?"

The shawl left Maggie's hand and wrapped itself around Jennifer. "You're right, I guess..." Jennifer's voice sounded less despairing.

Sam moved forward and put his arm around the shawl, then dropped it and just patted her on the back.

"And you've found out something," he said. "Your grandmother may be kidnapped, but she's obviously still alive. They can't use a dead hostage. She's here somewhere!"

"And," said Maggie. "We'd better retrieve those diamonds. Brady won't be able to bargain but we can. Come on, Jennifer. We'll go out the back way and come up on the side of the pyramid away from where he's watching, so you can keep your shoe and shawl on until we get there!"

They didn't dare use the flashlight, and once they got out behind the Nun's Quadrangle it was dark indeed. They stood awhile, letting their eyes adjust.

"Just make sure we stay away from the body..." Jennifer whispered. "You don't think they killed him because he didn't have the necklace?" Her voice was shaky again.

"Nope," Sam wasn't just trying to be nice and reassure her. "I'd be willing to bet they killed him because they were sure he *had* it! Then they found out he didn't. Too late."

Jennifer left them safely hidden in the little recess on the side of the pyramid where they'd hidden before and went to scout for guards. Maggie and Sam could hear her coming back. She was mumbling "Ouch! Ouch! Ouch!" with each step she took.

"Come on!" she said. "There's nobody out in front." There was excitement in her voice now. "We'll get the diamonds and climb up the pyramid. We can hide in the little temple near the top and watch from there."

As silently as they could, Sam and Maggie edged around the pyramid to the stairs. A white sandal could faintly be seen moving ahead of them. To Sam's surprise, more of the lights had been switched off. The Entrance buildings were darkened. The guards must be out in front. Maybe it was lunch or coffee break or something.

There was some scratching and then a flash of reflected light. Jennifer had found the necklace. She must be crouching down, for the diamonds seemed to drift along the ground toward them.

"Here, Maggie," the brilliant stones came up to Maggie's hand. "Put them on. If you do up the top button on your blouse they'll be hidden."

Sam watched the necklace fastened around Maggie's neck. Jennifer was right. It was a very good hiding place. As long as the Bad Guys didn't figure it out.

They climbed the pyramid fearfully, staying as far away from the entrance buildings as they could and still be on the steps. Once in a while they even had to dare to use the flashlight. They had finally reached the little temple building near the top when the guard in the woolen hat appeared below. Lunch break must be over.

He and Maggie tucked themselves back into a corner, but Señor Woolen Hat never looked up. He was wandering around the foot of the pyramid kicking at stones. That's about where Jennifer said Chita had dropped her purse. Not far from where Jennifer had just uncovered the necklace. Finally he gave up. Another guard came and joined him and they began to walk toward the Nun's Quadrangle.

"Should I go down and follow them?" Jennifer didn't sound too enthusiastic.

Sam remembered the "ouches" when she was walking back. "Why don't we climb the rest of the way to the top. It's not far. If we're quiet they won't look back...or up."

Silently, they managed. Sam wondered, as they settled themselves, what the guards would see if they did look up. The faint outline of two people, a shawl and a shoe? Would they even notice or believe? Maybe they'd think it was just the witch's magic come back to her son's pyramid.

Funny, he thought, as he kept his eyes focussed on the two guards – here he was, a phoney magician sitting on top of a real magician's temple. And even if the magic in the legend hadn't been real – there was real magic here now. Jennifer's invisibility magic was pretty powerful stuff.

If they had hoped that the guards would lead them to Mrs. Arnold, they were disappointed. The two men stood smoking and talking and then came back. Neither looked up as they went back into the entrance buildings.

**M**aggie wouldn't have missed this for the world. She could wish that she was here under different circumstances but how else would she be sitting at the top of a Mayan pyramid in the Yucatan when dawn broke over the jungle?

Far away she could hear the birds. Before the first glimmer of sunlight etched the sky there was the distant sound of birdsong. It rose and swelled louder and louder as it swept over the black treetops. The wave of sound flowed toward them ahead of the sun. It was magnificent. She would never forget it.

She knew there were tears on her cheeks. She dared a look at Sam. Awe and wonder. So that was what it looked like.

"Wow!" breathed Jennifer.

It took them a few minutes to compose themselves. Watching the far treetops go from black to green and the light spread as the sunlight lit the top of the Great Pyramid and the other buildings came into view was amazing. This time Jennifer was the practical one.

"Those guards are about due for another patrol," she said. "You two had better hide in the little temple, then when they go back in you can climb down." The sandal and shawl came at Maggie again. "I'll go down now and follow them. Meet you at the Nun's Quadrangle after they go back in."

They followed Jennifer "ouching" her way down the steps to the little temple. Then she was quiet. Guards were coming out. From up here Maggie couldn't tell if they were the same ones or not. Perhaps the shift had changed. Perhaps these guards would do a real patrol and not just take a smoke break at the top of the stairs and go back.

Now that it was light they would have been terribly exposed up here. Grand's black shawl would have shown up against the sand-coloured stonework of the pyramid. She tried to squeeze further out of sight. At least her beige shorts and sweater were sort of camouflage as she flattened herself against the stones. She looked over at Sam, who was doing the same thing. His khaki shorts and jacket were good too. Even his constant companion backpack matched. She fumbled at her throat. The necklace was hidden. She could imagine it flashing in the sun's rays like a beacon if she wasn't careful.

Either they were the same guards or they were using the same patrol system as the earlier ones because they were walking back. Maggie held her breath, but the men didn't look up, just walked slowly back up the steps to the turnstiles and buildings.

"You can breathe now." Sam was grinning at her.

Reluctantly, she moved. Looking down, she wondered how they'd ever made it up here in the dark. Maybe looking up and not being able to see below them had been a good thing.

Sam had already begun the descent. There were stair steps around the little temple, which made it better. They could turn around and descend more easily. Maggie only hoped that the guards would stick to their schedule and not come back before they managed to get to the Nun's Quadrangle where there were places to hide. She'd rolled the sandal up in Grand's black shawl and tucked it under her sweater. She was convinced the black would stand out against the stones and attract attention.

They were down at last. Now they ran and began the twisting climb up the steps to where they had sat for the show the night before.

"Look!" Sam pointed to a fresh smudge of blood on the step above him. "Jennifer's foot's bleeding. Those 'ouches' weren't for nothing!"

"Poor Jen," Maggie said. "Good thing the guards weren't as observant as you are."

They arrived at the chairs. The sandal was snatched out of Maggie's hand. "We'd better hurry and do a search before they come to remove these chairs and get the place ready to open." Jennifer's sandal had a smear of red on it as it moved away.

"Did they say anything?" Maggie followed the sandal. "Any clues as to where Grand was hidden?"

"Nope, but she's here somewhere. They said they'd 'uncover' her before Brady gets here. Whatever that means." The sandal stopped in front of the row of cells adjacent to the chairs. "We've got to find her before they come back. They're meeting Brady just after the site opens at six o'clock.

The tour buses start arriving around 8 or 9 a.m. and the place gets really busy." Jennifer's voice trailed off.

"Uncover?" Maggie turned to Sam, looking frightened. "They can't have buried her?"

"**N**o," Sam said. "I'm sure they wouldn't have buried her." He wished he'd thought of it sooner. He rushed ahead bumping into Jennifer. "There's some canvas and construction stuff in one of the little rooms. I saw it yesterday but last night we must have missed it. There!"

Now, in the daylight, he could see that the canvas was pulled away from the chicken wire and rubble it had been covering before. And it was moving.

"Grand!' cried Jennifer. Sam felt her pushing past him. The canvas was being pulled back.

Now Sam could see wrists tied together. The familiar silver bracelets Mrs. Arnold always wore were half-hidden by rope.

He and Maggie sprang forward to help Jennifer lift away the canvas.

She was covered in cement dust, but the eyes above the dirty cloth that was tied about her mouth were open and she looked to be okay. Maggie had pulled the rag away and removed the gag from her grandmother's mouth as Mrs. Arnold spat dust.

"Sam," she said, when at last she could speak, "I do hope you're still carrying that bottle of water in your backpack. I could certainly use a sip or two to clear out the taste of that filthy rag."

Sam just nodded and took off the backpack. He fumbled with the water bottle pocket. Thank goodness there was some water left. He held it to her mouth.

"Thank you, Sam," Mrs. Arnold said after she'd rinsed her mouth and spat the water into the pile of rubble beside her. She took a long drink before she spoke again. "Perhaps someone should keep a look-out?"

"I'll go." Jennifer's sandal paused at the door. "Love you, Grand!" There was relief in her voice.

"Oh, Grand!" Maggie was tugging at the ropes on the wrists as she spoke. "We've got to get you out of here."

Sam worked hastily on the knots at her ankles. He wished he had a knife, but at least the rope here was thicker and the knot was loosening. "If I can get this off we can help you up and you can walk, at least." He said. "Maybe we should just try to carry you out. Into another cell?" To his relief, he managed to undo the outer knot, wiggle the rest, and pull the rope away. "Here, Maggie," he said, "you can massage your grandmother's ankles and I'll work on that one."

He could hear the sound of Jennifer's sandals outside.

"Quick!" She said. "They're coming!" The sandal was in the doorway. "We've got to move you, Grand!"

Sam and Maggie helped Mrs. Arnold stand. "Can you walk?" He asked, "or are your feet too numb?"

"I think I can manage," she said, leaning on them as she began to hobble out. "Jennifer? Perhaps you could cause a distraction and delay them long enough for us to get down and hide in one of the rooms on the lower level."

The sandal left without a word. Sam could see it heading for the chairs as they hurried Mrs. Arnold to the steps on the other side. They were moving so slowly he feared they'd never make it. But then there was a sound of a rock crashing down the outer stairs and then another. Confused shouts, as it seemed a volley of rocks were going in all directions. Good for Jennifer, Sam thought. At last they reached the stairs. Mrs. Arnold was walking better now.

"Luckily," she said, "they didn't have enough of the thin rope to tie my feet and the thicker sort couldn't be tied as tight. I'm afraid though," she held her hands up in front of her, "we'll have to find a knife or something to get this off."

They were down the stairs now. Sam wondered if they could actually make it to the little arched doorway and get outside the courtyard altogether. The voices were getting closer now. Just as they reached one of the little cells on the bottom level he could see chairs on the level above being overturned, thrown back toward the men who had entered. And then as he watched from inside the room a white sandal came over the edge and fell onto the grassy space beyond them.

"Jennifer?" Maggie gasped. "Oh no! Jennifer!"

She stared in horror as the sandal lay where it had fallen, willing it to move. But it just lay there on its side, the sole facing toward the little cell-like room where she and Grand and Sam were hiding.

"She's okay," Sam said, though his tone wasn't as convincing as Maggie wished. "She's got to be okay."

The sandal remained as it was. Above them they could hear sounds of a scuffle. More chairs scraping along, one arced out over the courtyard and fell not far from the sandal. Still no movement.

And then someone in a guard's uniform came rushing into the courtyard through the archway that faced the ballcourt.

"Juan! *Llame a la policia! Hombre es muerte! Arriba!*"

The man didn't wait for a response but disappeared back through the doorway.

"Oh, oh," breathed Maggie. "They're calling the Police? About a man? What's *arriba*?"

"Yes," said Grand, "he just said to call the police about a

dead man. Obviously this guard isn't in with Juan up there. *Arriba*," she added, "just means hurry."

For a moment Maggie felt a glimmer of hope. If the guard there was calling the police about the body *he* obviously wasn't in with Juan. Then the hope died. "Those two we thought were fake guards must work here," she said ruefully. That means we'd be out of luck trying to get the real guards to help us"

Sam nodded, "I guess the regular guards have found that phoney janitor,"

"Jennifer's janitor is dead?" Grand didn't miss much.

Maggie was struggling with the ropes on Grand's wrists. "Umhum," she mumbled. "We found his body last night while we were looking for you. Stabbed."

Somehow, Maggie thought, the problems of the night seemed very far away now. They had to get Grand free and somehow get to Jennifer. Her neck was itching. She'd forgotten about the stupid necklace. It didn't matter now. If only Jennifer was all right. She didn't even want to look at the sandal lying motionless in the grass. She hoped that her sister had just thrown it over, but why was it lying on its side like that? Wouldn't it have landed flat if there was no foot in it? Still no movement. Jennifer would have been knocked out from the fall. If only that was all.

"Here," said Sam, pushing her away. "I'll work on the ropes for awhile." He'd found a piece of broken glass and began to rub it carefully across the binding. Maggie could see the fibres begin to part.

They could hear voices now. One of the two bad guy guards, probably Juan, was coming down from the level above them.

"I'd better go check so he doesn't come back again. You get the old lady and get her out of here."

Even though they were beneath the stairs they moved away from the entrance. Maggie could see the man heading out of the archway but he didn't go through. Just stood there staring out.

"Juan!" The voice came from above. "Get back up here! She's gone!"

Maggie pressed back out of sight as the man turned and began to run toward the stairs. She was afraid he'd have noticed movement, but he was looking up at his partner. She could hear running feet on the stone steps above her.

What could they do? The men would search the upper level and then come down here. Grand couldn't run – she was just beginning to walk okay. She looked at Sam. He was still scraping steadily at the ropes – halfway through. She admired his persistence. Maybe they could leave Grand here and run to the archway and draw the men away from their search. There would be other guards out by the body and police arriving soon. But the real guards knew Jose and would believe whatever he said. She felt hopeless.

"Very good, Sam!" Grand whispered as her hands came free. She rubbed her wrists, grimacing with the pain as the circulation began.

Sam looked at his watch. "The site is supposed to open in five minutes," he spoke so softly Maggie could barely hear him, "Brady is coming to meet those men. I think they were going to trade the diamonds for the drugs but they don't have the diamonds so they wanted to trade you instead."

Now they have nothing to trade, Maggie realized. Brady could be walking into a trap. Except, if they kept searching they'd not only have Grand again, they'd have us too. And the diamonds.

She could hear the men moving about above. Actually, when she peeked out she could see one of them searching along the row of cells behind the chairs. She ducked back, flattening herself against the wall.

"I doubt," whispered Grand, "if the police will allow them to open the site. A man has obviously been murdered. They can hardly call it suicide this time if, as you say Maggie, the knife was in his back."

Grand was right. Brady wouldn't be able to get in. And they couldn't get out. She'd counted on the press of crowds so that they would be able to leave. She had it all planned. They would retrieve the headsets from where she and Sam had hidden them, get Grand's driver's license, and be off. No chance of that now. They'd be found eventually. She wouldn't even think about that part.

And there was worse. Jennifer's sandal lay in front of her – deathly still.

Jennifer crouched at the far end of the row away from the two men. From here she could see the doorway of the little room below where Grand and Maggie and Sam were hidden. Now and then Maggie would take a peek out, but there was no way Jennifer could signal her.

Throwing the sandal over had probably been a bad idea but her foot was bleeding again and she was afraid that if the men found it and saw it was stained they'd know to look for bloody tracks. They'd never see her – but they could track her. Anyway she'd achieved her purpose of distracting them while Maggie and Sam moved Grand. For now, she could rest. Her foot was killing her.

The men had almost completed their search on this level. So at last she knew Señor Woolen Hat's name. Juan. He was moving methodically along the area where Grand had been hidden while the other man searched near Jennifer. She'd figured out why they were speaking English. The other man, Leroy, was definitely not Mexican. He had an American accent – Texas, she guessed. She hoped Brady would show up soon. Somehow, she'd have to get down to

Maggie and sneak the necklace to him though she hadn't quite figured out how she'd do it. She hoped he wouldn't bring the Señorita.

"Juan!" The other guard was back at the archway. *"¿Todo bien?"*

Jennifer could barely make out Maggie's beige shorts inside the little room. Get back, Maggie, she thought. But the man was looking up as Juan ran past her.

*"Sí!* Is all right!" he called. *"Un momento!* Come on," he called to the American, "you search below while I go outside and convince this guy to stay with the body."

No! Jennifer wasn't about to let anyone search down there. She picked up a chair and threw it into the doorway of one of the little rooms. Both men stopped on the stairs and ran back up.

They couldn't have seen anything, thought Jennifer. But the guard in the doorway was looking up in horror. Had he seen the chair lifting up, she wondered, or just looked when he heard the noise and saw it landing?

*"Madre de Dios!"* he said and fled.

The two men looked baffled, but they didn't search long. Once again they were heading down the stone steps. Jennifer got ready to grab another chair. And then Brady appeared.

There were a couple of men with him, but they didn't follow him as he came around the corner to confront the men on the stairs. He was wearing a plain beige sports shirt. It didn't look to Jennifer as if he was carrying a gun. But she could see that the two men behind him wore dark, official-looking jackets and their hands hovered in front as if ready to draw.

"Now you must tell me where to pick up the merchandise!"

Juan laughed in disbelief as he came up the stairs toward Brady. "Not until we receive payment!"

Jennifer was at the stairs now. She had moved as quickly as she could, but she couldn't get past the two men below her on the stairs. There was no way she could go down and retrieve the diamonds for Brady. She waited.

She had to hand it to Brady. He was playing it cool. "The drop was made last night," he said evenly, "payment was made. Where do I pick up the merchandise?"

"Y'all's kidding!" Leroy drawled, pulling a gun from inside his shirt.

Too late for Jennifer. She was standing at the top step between him and Brady. She tried to move back, but Brady had moved forward, blocking her. She couldn't get by without touching him. Maybe. If she crawled. At least, she thought, holding her breath as she crouched down, I'll be out of range – unless Leroy shoots low.

"Conchita made the drop." Brady said calmly. "If you didn't pick it up, who did?"

"Montero's man." Leroy's voice was threatening now. "But it wasn't in the purse when we got 'im."

Keep talking guys, thought Jennifer. As long as Brady's looking at you he won't notice the dust disturbed at his feet. She was starting to feel light-headed from holding her breath so long. At last she was far enough away. She stopped crawling and leaned against the stone wall. There wasn't much she could do now except try to sort out what was going on.

Brady had told them that Conchita's necklace was a payment from one gang to another. Diamonds for drugs, she figured. Brady was obviously pretending to be part of Conchita's gang so he could pick up the 'merchandise' and make a bust. But now it seemed there was another group involved.

Leroy was doing all the talking. "Look," he said, "no trouble. The merchandise is in the port at Progreso. Safely stowed...ready to go," he paused and waved the gun for emphasis, "when we get payment!"

Jennifer looked at Brady. He had the strangest expression on his face. At first she thought he was just trying not to look puzzled. She stood up and looked down into the courtyard.

To her horror Grand had stepped out from under the stairs. What could she be thinking?

Jennifer wondered how quickly she could crawl over and pick up a chair.

They could hear every word of what was going on above them. It sounded to Maggie as if Brady had reached some sort of a stalemate. He needed the diamonds but there was no way she could get them to him now. Absently she fingered the necklace at her throat. She hadn't realized Grand was watching and then her grandmother was undoing the top button.

"Stay here, Sam!" Grand whispered. "We might need you to run out to those Police and get help." With that she took Maggie by the arm and moved her out into the courtyard and stood her close to the wall out of sight. She, herself moved well out, in view of those above.

Maggie couldn't understand. What was Sam supposed to do? It was quite a distance to the archway exit. Grand must be out of her mind.

Peeking out from under the shadow of the stairs, Maggie could see Brady standing alone and unarmed at the top. Worse still she could see two men near the top of the steps and one of them had a gun. Grand seemed unfazed. Did she think Brady had a gun hidden somewhere?

"Mr. Brady!" Grand called.

Brady had already spotted her, but the men on the stairs spun around. The one with the gun now had it pointed at Grand. Maggie got ready to duck back into the room, but her grandmother stood firm.

"I'm assuming you're not alone?"

As if on cue one man appeared behind Brady. His gun was trained on the men on the steps.

"Surely this can be settled without gunfire?" Grand said calmly. "I believe the police are close by and would be upset to have another murder to deal with. So why," she spoke directly to the men on the stairs, "don't you just conclude the deal?"

Maggie realized it was her cue. She undid the clasp of the necklace, stepped out of her hiding place and waved the diamonds in the air. "Here you are Mr. Brady!" She threw the necklace as hard as she could. It arced upwards, flashing in the sunlight and landed beside the chairs. Before she could make another move Grand had yanked her back toward the room out of range of the guns.

Now she leaned against the doorway, expecting bullets to be whizzing by. There was no sound. The only person above that she could see was Brady as he moved over to retrieve the necklace.

"So," he said calmly, "where at the docks in Progreso did you say the goods were hidden?"

They could hear one of the men responding, but they could hear something else. Someone coming down a couple of steps and then leaping over the rest of the way, dodging under the overhang as he came toward them.

Maggie hadn't noticed anyone at the archway of the

courtyard until she saw a gun followed by a man in a dark jacket, who snapped out a command.

"Stop!" He ordered.

The man who'd jumped was close enough now that she realized it was Señor Woolen Hat. He wasn't armed, and she thought at first he might grab her, but Sam's hand came out of the doorway and snatched her away. The man stopped and slowly raised his hands.

And then it was over. Brady had flashed a badge and his men rounded up the two men while Maggie rushed over to Jennifer's sandal. To her relief it was empty. Quietly, she and Sam followed Grand up the stairs. Brady only nodded to them. "Thanks," he said and left.

Standing up here in the sunlight her grandmother looked exhausted. Very much like a woman who'd spent the night tied up under a canvas.

Sam spotted a smudge of blood on the stones nearby. "Maybe it's time to try to figure out a way to get Jennifer to laugh so we can get out of here."

"We definitely can't tickle her foot!" Grand said. "But I suppose you two will think of something."

It seemed to Sam now that working with his grandfather on the dig at Sayil was going to be a bit of a let-down after the excitement of the past few days.

He was still trying to figure everything out. Now that they were back at the hotel, he and Maggie and Jennifer had been able to piece things together. A little.

"So Brady wasn't really DEA after all?" Maggie said. "The whole drug thing was a cover?"

"Right," said Jennifer swishing her straw around in the tall lemonade she was drinking. "He wasn't after drugs. It was guns those diamonds were supposed to be buying."

They were sitting in the hotel restaurant. Mrs. Arnold had bathed and changed. Grandad had arrived to take Sam to the dig but had stayed to visit with the girls' grandmother while Sam said good-bye to Maggie and Jennifer. It hadn't turned out to be "good-bye" so much as trying to sort things out.

"So was the lovely 'Chita' one of the gang trying to buy the guns?" Maggie was watching for Sam's reaction as she said this. He could tell.

Sam shook his head. "I think," he said ignoring the tease, "that it was a little of both. I think she really was helping Brady, but they had to make it look as though he was forcing her to co-operate so it wouldn't blow *her* cover. Maybe because it was her job as an undercover agent, and maybe for revenge against Montero's gang for killing her partner." Sam remembered the tears in those beautiful brown eyes.

"Of course!" said Jennifer, giving Maggie a look and making loud slurping sounds.

"So Montero wanted the diamonds so the deal with Conchita would fall through," said Maggie, ignoring her. "But what would he have wanted those guns for? A rebellion somewhere?"

"Maybe." Sam wondered. "Maybe he really is a drug lord who wants to set up his own territory like those guys in Colombia."

He decided to change the subject. "What about the charming Greek tycoon? I guess that means he wasn't planning to smuggle drugs from Mexico to the U.S. but guns from the U.S. into Mexico."

Maggie shook her head. "I don't think so. Grand said that he was a sort of Plan B. If Brady didn't sort things out here, Montero's gang were going to hijack his yacht. And him."

"Oh?" Sam looked interested. "Is that why Alekos was there? Undercover for Brady?"

"I guess." Jennifer sighed. "It would be much simpler if they'd tell us things. For instance, why did Juan and Leroy think they needed a hostage? Brady would be giving them diamonds for the *merchandise* anyway. And why would they think he would be willing to trade for Grand? Wouldn't any other tourist have done?"

"I guess because they'd seen Grand arriving with him and talking to him a couple of times." Maggie shook her head.

"You don't think she was being too curious? You know...they thought she was in the way?" Jennifer grinned. "I may have to speak to her about that!"

"Okay, you two..." Sam leaned forward grinning, "have you decided what you're going to tell your mother?"

"Are you kidding? Nothing, nothing..." said Jennifer.

"*Nada*," laughed Maggie. "We had a lovely and very educational Spring Break."

"Slightly boring..." added Jennifer. "But the beaches were nice."

"Of course," Maggie sighed dramatically, "it would have been nicer if we'd got to keep the diamonds!"

Sam stared across the terrace to where Mrs. Arnold was sitting with his grandfather. They do make a lovely couple, he thought.

He and the girls watched as she took a sip of her drink and clutched her throat.

Jennifer gasped. He could see Maggie was panicking too.

"Quick, Maggie," Sam was already out of his chair. "How do you say 'doctor' in Spanish?"

Jennifer jumped up "We didn't rescue her just to have her poisoned before our very eyes."

Then they stopped where they were as Mrs. Arnold put her glass down and declared, "I swear this hotel makes the worst Margarita in Mexico!"

# ACKNOWLEDGEMENTS

**M**any thanks for my amazing (and most patient) editor Geoffrey Ursell. Special thanks to good friends Janice MacDonald and Randy Williams whose friend Dan climbed the Mayan pyramid in the dark and described the amazing dawn scene.

And to my faithful travelling companion (and wonderful husband) Earl Georgas for finding a place to hide the body!

photo: Benje Bondar

**C**ora Taylor is one of Canada's best-known children's authors, having published more than a dozen juvenile novels, including *Adventure in Istanbul*, the first book in the "Spy Who Wasn't There" series. She's also produced three titles in the "Ghost Voyages" trilogy and *The Deadly Dance* for Coteau. Other recent titles include *On Wings of Evil*, and the "Angelique" series.

Her books have won numerous awards, including the Canada Council Children's Literature Prize, the Canadian Library Association's Book of the Year Award, the Ruth Schwartz Book Award, and Alberta's R. Ross Annett Award for Children's Literature.

Cora Taylor was born and raised in Saskatchewan, moved to Edmonton in the 1950s, and studied writing with the likes of Rudy Wiebe and W.O. Mitchell. She currently divides her time between Edmonton, Ontario, and Florida.

# The Deadly Dance

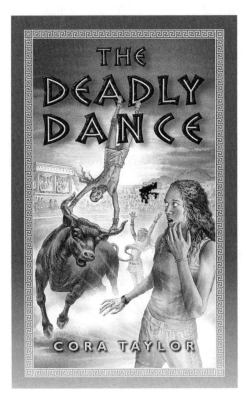

Trapped in ancient Crete, will Penny be able to learn the Deadly Dance in time?

1-55050-272-7
$8.95CAD/$7.95USD
Ages 12 & up